# Even Stephen

Curtis hung up and I stood holding the phone and smiling at it. I remembered a phrase that Stephen had learned in his Latin class: "mirabile dictu." It means "wonderful to say," and after he learned that phrase, Stephen used to walk into the house and say, "Mirabile dictu, I've been made one of the starters for the basketball team." Or, "Mirabile dictu, my teacher gave me an *A*-plus on that report I did for English." Most recently, it was, "Mirabile dictu, I got into Harvard!"

In all my life, I'd rarely had occasion to say "mirabile dictu." Now I felt like shouting those words out loud.

## By Johanna Hurwitz

*Make Room for Elisa*
*Much Ado About Aldo*
*New Neighbors for Nora*
*New Shoes for Silvia*
*Nora and Mrs. Mind-Your-Own-Business*
*Once I Was a Plum Tree*
*Ozzie on His Own*
*The Rabbi's Girls*
*Rip-Roaring Russell*
*Roz and Ozzie*
*Russell and Elisa*
*Russell Rides Again*
*Russell Sprouts*
*School's Out*
*School Spirit*
*Spring Break*
*Starting School*
*Superduper Teddy*
*Teacher's Pet*
*Tough-Luck Karen*
*The Up & Down Spring*
*A Word to the Wise: And Other Proverbs*
*Yellow Blue Jay*

# EVEN STEPHEN

### ❖ *Johanna Hurwitz* ❖

*illustrated by Michael Dooling*

**BEECH TREE**
New York

Another version of chapter 7 was previously published in *The Lost Treasure* by Scholastic Inc., copyright © 1987. Reprinted with permission.

Text copyright © 1996 by Johanna Hurwitz
Illustrations copyright © 1996 by Michael Dooling

Published by Morrow Junior Books
a division of William Morrow and Company, Inc.
1350 Avenue of the Americas, New York, NY 10019
www.williammorrow.com

Printed in the United States of America.

The Library of Congress has cataloged the Morrow Junior Books edition of *Even Stephen* as follows:
Hurwitz, Johanna.
Even Stephen / Johanna Hurwitz.
p. cm.
Summary: A traumatic event in the lives of seventeen-year-old Stephen and his fourteen-year-old sister helps them to understand and accept themselves and each other.
ISBN 0-688-14197-8
[1. Self-acceptance—Fiction.  2. Brothers and sisters—Fiction.]  I. Title.
PZ7.H9574Ev 1996  [Fic]—dc20  95-17987  CIP AC

First Beech Tree Edition, 1998
ISBN 0-688-16362-9
10 9 8 7 6 5 4 3 2 1

*Because we're old friends,*
*And because I love*
*Carol, Sam, Pam, and David Baron,*
*Here is a book for them.*

# Contents

# EVEN STEPHEN

# ONE
## ❧ *Playing Dead* ❧

HERE'S ONE OF the best compliments I ever got. It came from Carly Rustin, who is three years old. She told it to me one evening when I was baby-sitting.

"I love your hair," she said, stroking it as we sat side by side and I read a bedtime story to her. "It's just like my Honey's." Honey is her dog—a golden retriever.

"I've got hair like a dog, a face like a frog, and a brain that's the size of a pea," I told my mother.

"Allison Marx, stop that at once," she scolded when she heard me. Mom only calls me Allison when she is annoyed. Usually, she calls me Sunny. "Your hair is beautiful. And don't you dare belittle yourself."

"Be little? I couldn't be little if I wanted. I'm taller than just about every girl I know," I complained.

"Oh, Sunny." She gave me a hug. "You're beautiful, and you're my favorite daughter! The very best one I have," she insisted.

Of course, I am also her only daughter, so she's not saying much. It's nice to have her champion my hair, which is my one good point. Still, I noticed she didn't mention my face and my eyeglasses. She didn't remind me that I can hardly carry a tune, follow directions, or keep up with my class in algebra. I'm not like my brother, Stephen, at all.

"Hold still," Stephen said to me one day last winter. "Remember, you're supposed to pretend to be dying."

"I'm trying," I answered, choking back a giggle. My five-foot-eight-inch body was lying facedown on the floor in our living room. The carpeting tickled my nose, and I thought I would sneeze at any moment. Playing dead is not as easy as you would think.

"Wake up. Wake up," Stephen shouted in my ear as he turned me over and shook my shoulders roughly. My glasses slipped down my nose.

Then I really couldn't help it. I started laughing as I sat up and adjusted my glasses. "I *am* awake, silly," I pointed out. "Why are you shouting for me to wake up? You told me to act like I had fainted or died or something morbid like that. You've got to make up your mind."

Stephen grinned at me. "That's the first step in CPR," he said apologetically. "If I don't practice this stuff I just learned, I won't remember how to do it. Mr. DeAngeli, the instructor, said it was important that we review all the steps at home so that they become second nature."

"How did you practice in the class?" I asked him.

"We had dummies made out of plastic. And they didn't laugh," he said, giving me a poke in the ribs.

"If I was made out of plastic, I wouldn't laugh, either," I reminded him.

Stephen is seventeen, three years older than me. Just about every kid I know hates the brothers or sisters, or, at the very least, only tolerates them. It's not like that with Stephen and me. We're good friends and always have been. He almost never nags or teases me. He's even trained his girlfriends to be nice to me. So if Stephen asks me to lie down and pretend I'm dying, of course I'll do it for him.

"Let's start over," I suggested, rubbing my nose. "I'll try to be more serious this time."

"Thanks, Sunny," said Stephen. "Maybe someday I'll save someone's life. This could be very important."

I rested my head back on the floor and through half-closed eyes I looked up at Stephen. His hair is blond, but a darker shade than mine. We both have blue eyes, which we inherited from our mom. Lucky Stephen has twenty-twenty vision, while I have to wear glasses, like Dad. And Stephen has a pair of dimples. If I suck in my breath and try to smile, I can create a half dimple. But the expression on my face is so weird that I've only tried it in the mirror when no one was looking.

This time when Stephen shouted in my ear, "Wake up. Wake up," I didn't laugh or even move. "Call nine-one-one," Stephen yelled to some invisible person over his shoulder. He pressed his fingers on my throat. "I'm taking your pulse," he explained to me.

Then he began tipping my head back, and he pressed down on my middle. Peeking through my half-closed eyes, I marveled at his concentration. For the moment, Stephen seemed to have forgotten that I was his kid-sister. I had become a victim who was in need of rescue.

"This is the point where I would give you mouth-

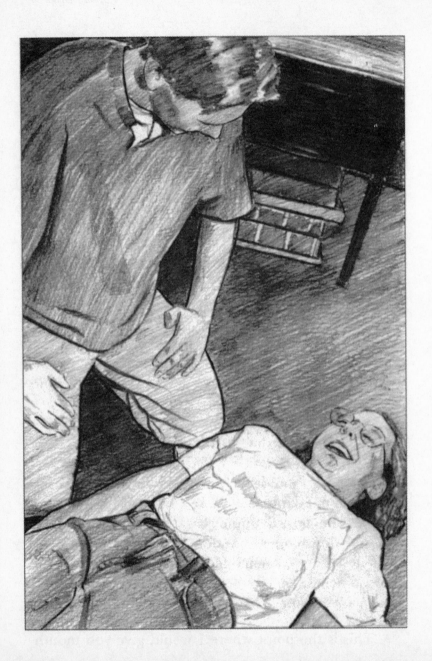

to-mouth resuscitation if you weren't breathing," Stephen explained.

The thought of receiving the "kiss of life" from Stephen made me start giggling all over again. I sat up. "Suppose I had just eaten a whole onion?" I asked him. "Would you still have to do it, even if I had bad breath?"

"Don't be silly. You don't think about bad breath when someone's dying," said Stephen.

"What about garlic?" I asked. "I read that some people eat whole cloves of garlic the way you and I eat potato chips. Their breath must really be gross."

"You've got halitosis on the brain," said Stephen.

Then I thought of something more serious. "Don't you have to worry that you might endanger yourself, doing that to someone you don't know?" I asked, shuddering at the thought. "You know, with AIDS and everything, it's probably not a good thing to do."

Stephen stood up for a moment and dug into his pocket. He is six foot three, so I had to really crane my head back to see his face. He removed his key ring from his pocket. "Look at this," he said, holding it out to me. "In this tiny plastic container on my key ring, there is a mask that I can use. Isn't that neat?"

"What about a toilet plunger?" I asked him. "Didn't we hear on the news that they discovered that pressing a toilet plunger against a victim's chest was even more efficient than this method you're using on me?"

"Yeah. Mr. DeAngeli told us about that. He even demonstrated how to do it. The problem is, people don't usually walk around carrying toilet plungers."

"Oh, Stephen," I said, laughing. "I'd love to see you walking to school carrying a toilet plunger." It was such a funny image. "You'd be even more popular than you are now. You could help the janitor when you weren't practicing basketball or taking a class or saving a life."

"Come on, Sunny," said Stephen, grinning. I guess he realized how funny it would be if people walked around carrying their own toilet plungers wherever they went.

"The plunger method works great but probably won't be put into use very often. On the other hand, unless I'm in the shower or something, I'm almost never without my keys."

"That's true," I agreed.

Stephen got back down on the floor and resumed "saving" my life.

I confess that from time to time I feel a twinge of jealousy toward my brother. He's so perfect at everything, while I'm just a so-so student, kind of average in most things I try to do. There is absolutely nothing average or ordinary about Stephen. Every teacher in the high school says he is *extraordinary,* the exceptional student, the exceptional human being. I'm already thinking of how I'm going to miss Stephen when he goes off to college in the fall.

It's not just because he's been working hard to help me get through algebra. I am truly in awe of my brother and have been since I was old enough to know who he was. There is absolutely nothing he can't do, and do easily and well—whether it's fixing the earpiece when it fell off my glasses, or helping me improve my swimming stroke in the summer, or teaching me to program the VCR or use our computer. He can do anything. So I'm confident that if anyone can get me through algebra, it's Stephen. But more than that, he's loads of fun. We always laugh when we're together. No wonder he's so popular at school. Of course, it doesn't hurt that he's the top scorer on the basketball team. He's also editor in chief of the *Hoover Herald,* our school paper, and he probably could have been elected president of the senior class, if he had wanted to run for it.

Stephen is always setting new goals for himself. No one told him to take the CPR course. It's just another thing he thought he should do. When he heard that no one in the history of Herbert Hoover High School had ever gotten a perfect score on the SAT exams, he took the exams twice. The first time he got 780 in math and 740 in English, out of a possible 800 on each test. Those scores automatically put him in the top 1 percent in the country. That wasn't good enough for Stephen.

And so he studied and took the tests again. I wasn't the least bit surprised when he was notified that he had gotten 1600—a perfect math test and a perfect English one. Of course, he's number one in the graduating class. On his college applications, he wrote essays about the thirty-first president of the United

States: Herbert Hoover. He defended Hoover's image and told about all the things he accomplished while he was in office. And he explained that the stock market crash of 1929 and the Great Depression that followed were events that were just waiting to happen. It was research Stephen had done for himself, not for any history assignment.

I wasn't the least bit surprised when Stephen was accepted *early action* at Harvard last December. It was another first in the history of our high school. Other students have been admitted to Harvard, but no one before had ever gotten such an early acceptance. Stephen was thrilled, and Mom and Dad and I were very proud of him. But two days later, I discovered him filling out more college applications.

"How many colleges can you attend?" I asked him. It seemed ridiculous that he was applying elsewhere once he had gotten into Harvard.

"I want to see if I can get into Yale and MIT and Princeton," he said. "I'm applying to Haverford, too." That's where Dad went to school.

"What's the point?" I asked. It seemed like such a waste of time to me—and expensive. You have to pay a fee to each college where you send an application. But for Stephen, one acceptance was not enough. He wanted every major college in the country to accept him. There was no doubt in my mind that he'd get into them all, too. But it seemed strange to me that Stephen felt the need to collect all those acceptance letters.

There's also no doubt in my mind that someday everyone will have heard of Stephen Marx. Whatever he does in the future, he'll do well. I know that eventually he'll be as famous, and better loved, than all those other people who just happen to share our last name: Karl and Groucho and Harpo and Chico. So even if all the good genes somehow went to him, I know I'm lucky to have my own Marx brother, Stephen.

Yet sometimes I find myself wondering what it must feel like to be as perfect as Stephen—to know that you can achieve anything you want, to have no limits to your ability. I envy that.

# TWO
## ❖ *The Leap Year Dance* ❖

IF STEPHEN'S STRENGTHS are his ability in basketball, his good looks, his sense of humor, and his perfect grades in algebra, geometry, calculus, biology, chemistry, physics, social studies, English, French, and Latin, I have an academic strength, too. At least I thought I did until I entered Mrs. Carson's freshman English class.

Mrs. Carson has a comma fixation. She wants commas where there are none, and she removes commas wherever she sees them. There's a saying about not being able to see the forest for the trees. Well, Mrs. Carson hasn't been able to see the point of anything I've written all year because she's been so busy looking at commas. I used to think I was a good writer. Now I'm no longer so sure.

In my spare time, I often write stories and poems, but nowadays I don't let anyone read them. I'm too afraid people will laugh and criticize what I have to say. I don't want anyone looking for missing commas! I know I'm not perfect like Stephen. Unlike when my brother tackles something, the pieces I write never turn out quite the way I want them to. Still, having a brother who is editor in chief of the school paper, I could have gotten a position as a junior reporter. In fact, when I entered high school last fall, Stephen asked me about signing up. But I was sure everyone would think the only reason I was on the paper was because of my brother. One Marx on the *Hoover Herald* was enough, I decided, so I declined. But still, I think some of the things I write are kind of good. However, since I'm terrified of finding out that they're not, I keep them hidden in a box in the back of my closet.

My mom is an elementary school teacher. She started teaching fourth grade when I entered first. Now I'm in high school and Mom is still in fourth grade. By now, she must be the world's best fourth grade teacher. She should be, after all this time. My dad is a lawyer. Stephen is thinking about becoming a lawyer, too. Dad said they can be partners.

"You go to law school and you can also be our partner," suggested Stephen. "We'll be Marx and Marx and Marx."

"I don't think I've got the *marks* to get into law school," I told Stephen. Besides, I don't want to be a lawyer. I'm not at all sure what I'd really like to be. Sometimes I think maybe I'd like to be a writer when I finish school. But I don't know if I'll ever be brave enough to show my writing to anyone.

Just now, however, I can't worry about the future. I have to work my way through the present. For me, the present means a passing grade in algebra. I wouldn't object to having a boyfriend, either. Why is it they are both so hard for me to attain?

Stephen helps me with algebra. Although he has loads of patience, it comes so easily for him, I can tell he doesn't understand why I'm having problems. I just don't have the math gene.

As for a boyfriend, that seems hopeless, too. You'd think having an older brother with lots of friends should make it easy for me. But I seem to be invisible to all his friends. They don't even know I exist. It must be another missing gene.

This is a leap year, and it seems in the olden times, when women just sat around helplessly waiting for men to ask them for dates or for marriage, a tradition grew up. During leap year, women were *allowed* to be more aggressive. They pursued the men. Since February 29 fell on a Saturday this year, someone at school got the idea of making a dance on that date open to the entire school, so even a freshman like me could hope to go. All the girls were supposed to ask the guys. So all I needed was to invite a boy to be my date. It sounds simple, but nothing is ever simple for me.

I wanted to ask Curtis Silvers. I've had a crush on him for over a year. Curtis is on the basketball team with Stephen. So naturally he's tall, which I like, being taller than half the kids my age. Curtis has drop-dead good looks, too: dark wavy hair that's always falling into his eyes and a wonderful smile. He looks like he should be a movie or TV star.

Even though he comes over to our house often, I didn't think he'd ever noticed me. I decided that the dance would be the perfect opportunity to introduce him to the other member of the Marx family who goes to his school. It took daring on my part. I thought about phoning him, but I knew that I'd choke to death before I could get the words out of my mouth.

I discussed the situation with my best friend, Ellie. "You could pass him a note," she suggested. "We see him eating lunch when we're in the cafeteria."

"I don't want to put it in writing," I said, horrified at her idea. "In the first place, he might not even remember who I am when he sees my name. There are so many people in the school. In the second place, if he throws the note away, someone else could find it and read it. That would be mortifying."

"In the third place, maybe he doesn't know how to read," said Ellie, teasing me. "You're just looking for excuses. You have to act. It's not going to happen magically."

Ellie already had a date for the dance. She was going with a boy named Mike who sits next to her in Spanish. He's an inch shorter than she is, even though she's not nearly as tall as I am.

"I'm not going to marry him," Ellie reminded me. "But he's easy to talk to and I want to go to the dance. Go on, be brave. What's the worst thing that Curtis can say to you?"

"I can't take rejection," I told her.

"He's only another high school student. If he tells you no, it's his loss. Ask him, Sunny."

So when Stephen mentioned that Curtis was coming over after school to practice shots with him, I took my brother into my confidence.

"I want to ask Curtis to the Leap Year Dance," I said. "What should I do?"

"You'll have to ask him," said Stephen, shrugging his shoulders. "Unless you've been secretly studying telepathy."

"You're no help," I complained. Stephen had already accepted one invitation and turned down two others. I felt sorry for the girls he had turned down.

"What did Nancy Cummings say to you?" I asked.

"She said, 'Stephen, all my life I have dreamed of having this wonderful opportunity. Will you please make me the happiest girl in the universe by accompanying me to the Leap Year Dance?' "

"Oh, come on, Stephen," I begged. "Be serious. What did she really say? What should I say?"

"She just said, 'Would you like to come to the Leap Year Dance with me?' And I said, 'Sure.' "

"And what about the girls you turned down? What did you say to them?" I wanted to know. I thought I might as well be mentally prepared for a negative response.

"I told them thanks for asking but said I'd already accepted another invitation."

"Will you leave me alone with Curtis for about twelve seconds?" I asked my brother. "That should be enough time for me to ask him and for him to refuse me."

"Don't be so negative," said Stephen. "I'll give you

fourteen seconds, and I bet he says yes."

So there I was in my red down jacket, hanging around watching Stephen and Curtis aiming shots into our old basketball hoop. "I'll be right back," Stephen called out to Curtis, and he went into the house. Curtis probably thought my brother had a call of nature. At least that's what I hoped. I didn't want him to think we'd set him up.

It took me a few moments to gather my nerve. My heart was beating rapidly and my mouth felt dry. I had to lick my lips and swallow a couple of times before I was ready.

"Say, Curtis," I called out, coming closer. "Do you have a date for the Leap Year Dance? You know, on February twenty-ninth. Will you go with me?"

Curtis stopped midshot and turned to look at me. "I'm Stephen's sister," I reminded him. "My name's Allison, but my brother and all my friends call me Sunny. I see you around school a lot. And, of course, I go to almost all the basketball games."

"Oh, hi," said Curtis. I don't know if he recognized me or not. Of course, I don't go around school wearing my down jacket. I pulled the hood off my head so he could see my face better. I wanted him to see my hair, too.

Maybe it was cheating on my part. How could Curtis tell me no when Stephen was walking out of the house, toward him? (I guess my fourteen seconds were up.) But taking advantage of one's position and good timing are two of the basketball skills that

Stephen has developed. So I used them, too.

"Well, uh, uh, uh, all right," mumbled Curtis, turning as red as my jacket.

"Great," I said, and ran back into the house before he could change his mind.

Curtis and my brother continued to play ball, and I started counting the days until the dance. There were twenty-two days to go. I savored every moment of those days. Even when I saw Curtis in the school hall and he blushed and went in the opposite direction, I didn't mind. I felt that when we were together, without my brother and without all the other students around, he'd get to know me and that maybe he'd even like me a little bit.

Stephen was amused. "Curtis isn't a great talker," he warned me. "His real strength is basketball."

"Maybe he'll find me more interesting to talk to than you," I teased him.

"I can't believe you really asked him," Ellie said. That was silly, because she was the one who had encouraged me to do the asking in the first place.

Often on Saturday evenings, I baby-sit. A woman named Mrs. Andrews phoned and asked if I could stay with her daughter, Sophie Rose, on the evening of the twenty-ninth. I told her I was busy. Then I got a call from Mrs. Rustin. She's the wife of Teddy Rustin, the phys ed teacher at the high school. He is also the coach of the basketball team.

"Sunny, will you be free to baby-sit for Carly a week from Saturday?" she asked. "My husband volunteered us to be chaperons at the high school's Leap Year Dance," she explained.

"I'm sorry, but I can't," I told her. "I'm going to the dance, too. I have a date," I reported proudly. "I'll see you there."

"I should have guessed you were going," said Mrs. Rustin. "I knew a pretty girl like you wasn't going to be free on Saturday evenings for long."

It was nice of her to call me pretty, but two weeks later as I was getting ready for the dance, I stared at my reflection and wondered how I would look to Curtis.

I was wearing a new turquoise dress that matched my eyes, if you looked underneath my glasses and noticed things like that. My mother had helped me make a French braid. I wear dresses so seldom, and with my hair in a new style, I almost felt like a different person. I hoped Curtis would appreciate the change.

Even though it was a girl-invite-boy kind of affair, the guys were expected to pick up the girls at their homes in the traditional way.

"See you at the dance," Stephen said when he left the house to pick up Nancy Cummings. He gave me the thumbs-up sign and grinned at me.

"Right," I said. My stomach was feeling jittery from nerves. I wondered if Nancy felt that way waiting for Stephen.

The dance was scheduled to begin at 8:30. I was expecting Curtis at 8:00. He wasn't at our house at

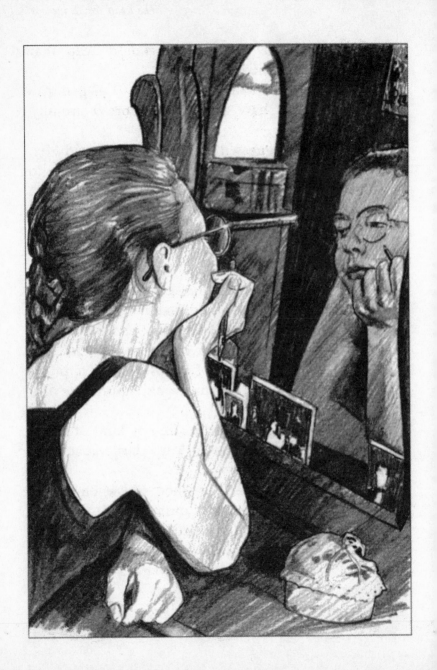

8:00 or 8:10 or 8:15 or 8:20. "Maybe he forgot the way," said my dad.

I guess he meant that as a joke. How could Curtis get lost when he'd been to our house a hundred times before?

"Maybe he's sick," Mom suggested.

That was a possibility. But wouldn't he have phoned to tell me? Well, I suppose he couldn't if he was very sick.

I wished that my parents had gone out for the evening. I didn't really need witnesses to this anxious wait for Curtis. On the other hand, I guess it was fortunate for me that it wasn't an evening when my mom and dad had guests. Sometimes on a Saturday night, they have people over to play bridge or for dinner. A bigger audience would have been worse.

I turned the pages of a magazine and pretended I wasn't looking at my watch every other minute. It became 8:30, then 8:45. By 9:00 I knew there was no way I could avoid phoning Curtis's home. I went to the telephone and dialed his number (which I had memorized weeks before).

A woman answered the phone. I guessed it was his mother. "Hello. Is Curtis there?" I asked.

"He's not here just now," she said.

"Is he on his way to my house?" I asked.

"Who is this?" the woman wanted to know.

I identified myself. "I'm Stephen Marx's sister. I invited Curtis to the Leap Year Dance at school. He said he'd take me. The dance has already started," I pointed out.

"Oh, dear, that's too bad," said the woman. "He went with his cousin to Pennsylvania early this morning. They were supposed to be back in time for supper. But in the late afternoon, he phoned to say they were having car trouble. They made it to a garage, but they were going to be delayed. I'm not sure when he'll get home. It might be any minute, though," she added.

"Oh," I said. What could I say?

I hung up and the phone rang almost immediately. I picked it up eagerly. "Sunny? Where are you? Are you okay?" It was Ellie.

"Curtis went off with his cousin, and they had a little car problem," I said. "So I guess we're going to be late."

"Going to be late? You are late already," said Ellie. She lowered her voice. "Did he stand you up?'

"No, no, nothing like that, honest," I said, wondering if that was true or not.

"Well, okay," said Ellie. "I just worried when I didn't see you here. Mike's an awful dancer," she whispered into the phone. "But he's got a good sense of humor, and it's fun to see everyone dressed up. The refreshments don't look that great. I already had a cup of very watery punch. I'm trying to keep away from the potato chips."

"I'll probably be there in a little while," I told her before we hung up.

"Why don't I take you to the dance?" Dad said, coming over to me and putting his arm around my shoulders.

I pulled away and I looked at him, horrified. How could I go to a high school dance with my father? I would never live it down if I lived to be a hundred.

The telephone rang again. "That's Curtis!" I shouted out happily, and picked up the receiver.

"Sunny? What's up?" asked Stephen.

I had never been so disappointed at hearing my brother's voice before in my life. "Curtis got held up. He drove somewhere with his cousin, and the car broke down. But he'll be here soon," I said, trying to sound more confident than I felt.

"I'll come and get you," offered Stephen. "Nancy and I will come together and bring you here."

"Oh no, Stephen," I said. "I'd rather wait for Curtis."

The doorbell rang. "There's the door," I shouted into the phone. "It must be Curtis. I'll see you in a little while." I banged down the telephone and rushed to the door, which my father had just opened. It was not Curtis. Curtis is six foot four, so imagine my shock when I saw this tiny little man with almost no hair at the door. Well, I guess he wasn't tiny. He was almost my height, and I certainly never think of myself as small. But if you're expecting someone six foot four, five seven looks like a midget. And even if he wasn't a midget, it was true that he didn't have much hair on his head.

"Hello?" my dad asked, puzzled. Neither of us recognized the man. And it's unusual for someone to come selling something at your door at that hour on a Saturday night.

The man held out his hand. "How do you do," he said. "I'm Robert Silvers, Curtis's father."

"Did you hear from Curtis again?" I asked him. "Is he okay?" Maybe he'd been in an accident, I worried.

"No. But I do feel bad about your not getting to the dance on time. And so I came to take you myself. My wife and I thought that would be a good plan. Then whenever Curtis comes home, he can take my place."

I looked at the little man. Ellie had a small date, but at least he went to high school. I just wouldn't be caught dead with small, bald Mr. Silvers.

"Well, uh, uh," I stammered. How could I make him understand how I felt? "I think I'd rather just stay home," I said weakly.

"Come in," my father invited Mr. Silvers. "Would you like a cup of coffee?"

Mr. Silvers came inside. I looked at him, searching for a resemblance to Curtis.

"I was just going to suggest that we play a fast game of Scrabble," my mother said. "It would make the time pass quickly for you, while you're waiting. How about it, Sunny?"

The last thing I felt like doing in my new dress was to sit around and play Scrabble. But at least it gave me a good excuse for not going to the dance with little Mr. Silvers.

"I guess so," I said without much enthusiasm.

So there we were: my parents, Curtis's dad, and me, playing Scrabble at 9:30 on Saturday night, February 29. It was a date that came around only once every four years. And this was one February 29 I would never forget. It was so terrible that it was funny!

It was my turn first. I looked at the seven Scrabble tiles I had before me and discovered I could take out my frustration by using my letters to make words that showed my mood. So I started off the game by making *H-O-R-R-I-D* (twenty-eight points because the *H* was on a double letter and the score was doubled because I was first). On my next move, I got only four points for spelling *N-U-T-S*.

"That's a waste of the letter *S*," my mother pointed out. The fourth grade teacher was at work, even on the weekend. "And you really ought to hold on to the *U* in case you pick up a *Q* before the game is out."

I shrugged my shoulders. I really wasn't as involved in this game as she was, that's for sure.

After her next turn, my mother got up for a couple of minutes and made some popcorn in the microwave.

When it was my turn again, I used all seven of my letters at once, spelling out *S-N-O-W-S-H-O-E* by connecting my letters onto the *S* that I had put down on the board before. It was the first time in all my years of Scrabble playing that I went out with all my letters. I got loads of points and was feeling better about life. Imagine a silly word game being able to do that to you.

"Sunny, that's brilliant," my mother exclaimed. I

beamed at her proudly. It *was* brilliant, I thought, chewing on a mouthful of popcorn.

"Wow, you're way ahead of all of us," Dad said, adding up my score.

After that, the game went quickly, because there were four players. We were just finishing up the game and picking over the unpopped kernels of corn in the bottom of the bowl when the doorbell rang. I looked at the clock. It was 10:45.

"I'll get it," I shouted, jumping up. Believe it or not, for a few minutes, I had actually forgotten about the dance and Curtis's standing me up.

"That's Curtis!" said Mr. Silvers, looking relieved. He was a novice Scrabble player and had struggled hard to keep up with the rest of us.

It wasn't Curtis. It was Ellie and Mike. A minute later, my brother and Nancy arrived. "This is beginning to look like a party," said Mr. Silvers.

"It is a party," said Stephen. He held up a large paper bag. "Nancy and I stopped and bought ice cream for everyone."

I felt like crying. It was so sweet of Stephen to buy that ice cream. He was trying to distract me from this stupid, crazy evening. And now everyone was here at my house. Everyone except Curtis, I thought. I didn't know whether to be annoyed at him or embarrassed. I had impressed all my friends by telling them that he was my date for the dance. How could I show my face at school on Monday after such a humiliating experience? And what about telling Mrs. Rustin that I couldn't baby-sit because I was going to the dance?

The doorbell rang again. This time, it actually was Curtis. He was wearing a pair of faded and torn jeans and an old jacket. There was grease on his face and his hands were black. He was obviously not dressed for a party. But if his cousin's car hadn't really broken down, he certainly had made himself look as if it had.

"Uh, hi," he said when he saw me. "I guess you heard all about the carburetor and everything."

"Yeah." I nodded, waiting for Curtis to say he was sorry. I guess he felt it was the carburetor that owed me an apology, because he didn't say anything more.

"You're too late for the dance, but you're just in time for ice cream," Stephen told his friend.

So Stephen and Nancy and Ellie and Mike and my parents and Mr. Silver and Curtis and I sat around the table with dishes of ice cream. We asked Curtis about the car. Stephen was right. He wasn't a big talker. And I really couldn't follow what he did say about the malfunctioning car parts. But at least Ellie heard the story, too. On Monday, she could back me up when I explained to everyone what had happened.

I wondered if Curtis would call and ask me out. Even with the grease smudge on his face, he looked handsome. I hoped he'd want to make it up to me. Despite everything, I still had a crush on him. And it seemed to me he owed me something for my evening of disappointment. I'd have to wait and see.

Curtis didn't phone the next day. But in the late

afternoon, I sat down and wrote a short story about it. I didn't worry about my commas, and somehow, describing the events made me feel better. Now it's hidden in the box in my closet. I wonder if I'll ever share it with anyone.

# THREE
## ❖ *Baby-sitting* ❖

IT'S GOOD THAT most Saturday nights don't contain the same level of drama as that last Saturday of February. The high and low caused by my expectation and disappointment were exhausting. It's much easier to follow my usual pattern of Saturday night baby-sitting.

Ellie hates baby-sitting. She says she feels nervous alone in someone else's home.

"You're not alone," I reminded her. "What about the child or children you're taking care of?"

"They're asleep," she complained. "At least, if I'm lucky, they're asleep. Otherwise, they're awake and driving me crazy." She crossed her eyes for emphasis.

"But you're not alone in the house," I said, laughing at her expression.

"It's a no-win situation," Ellie explained. "I want the children to go to sleep so I can do my homework or watch television or read a good book. But if they do fall asleep, then I start hearing all sorts of sounds: creaks on the stairs, the wind blowing through the chimney flue, the motor of the refrigerator in the kitchen, the thud of their cat jumping off a bed. None of it is really mysterious, but I begin to imagine all kinds of awful things. I can't wait to have the parents come home so I can get away from it all."

I don't feel that way. Usually, I love baby-sitting. In the first place, I think it's fun to have a chance to visit in someone else's home. I don't really snoop around, but it's interesting to see what foods they have in the refrigerator. (The first time I ever saw artichokes was at the Andrews's house.) And I like to see how people furnish their homes. I imagine how I would move the sofa and the chairs about if it was my house. I check out the books on their shelves and study the photographs on the mantelpiece. I guess it makes me seem nosy, but I love the chance to walk temporarily into someone else's setting.

In the second place, and of course, much more important, I love little kids. My mom says I'd make a great elementary school teacher, because I'm patient and caring. I don't want to hurt her feelings, but the truth is, I know I'd die if I had to spend my whole adult life back in school the way she does.

"Maybe she'll have two or three of her own children, one of these days," my dad suggested when he overheard me telling Mom that teaching's not for me.

"Stop that at once," my mother said, pretending to be annoyed. "I'm much too young to become a grandmother. And besides, Sunny has a lot of living to do before she becomes a parent."

"Don't worry, Mom," I promised. "Baby-sitting satisfies my maternal needs for the moment." And it does.

So there I was that first Saturday evening in March, back into my old routine, sitting with Carly Rustin, the little girl who compared my hair to that of her dog!

Most of the time when I arrived at the Rustins' home, Carly was at the door to greet me. Usually, she was holding an armload of books that she wanted me to read. They are old favorites of mine, too. Titles like *Madeline; Lyle, Lyle Crocodile;* and *Corduroy*. But that evening, I could hear Carly crying as Mr. Rustin opened the door for me. The Rustins' dog wagged her tail when she saw me. At least she was pleased by my arrival.

"Carly's having a bad day," Mr. Rustin said, shaking his head. "She's been whining off and on all day long."

"Hi, Carly," I called out when I caught sight of her. "I've got something for you in my pocket." I took out a lollipop. But Carly didn't reach for it.

"You're wearing my favorite pajamas tonight," I said.

Carly stopped crying for a moment and looked down at her pajamas. They were blue, with little red and green and yellow fish swimming all over them.

The distraction lasted only a second, because she threw her arms around her mother and began crying again. "Don't go. Don't go."

Mrs. Rustin bent down and gave her daughter a hug.

"Mommy and Daddy are just going out for a little while. You and Sunny always have a good time together. And Daddy and I will be back when you wake up in the morning," she said.

"No, don't go," sobbed Carly.

"I don't know what's gotten into her today." Mrs. Rustin sighed. "I hope this isn't the beginning of a new phase of clinging behavior. I wonder if she is coming down with something. I took her temperature a little while ago, and it was normal. This is just not like her."

"Don't worry." I tried to reassure Carly's mother. "She'll probably be fine after you go."

"We're just going to a movie. We won't be out late," said Mr. Rustin.

Mr. Rustin helped his wife put on her winter coat. Carly stood screaming in protest. "There's ice cream in the freezer," Mrs. Rustin said. "Help yourself, and Carly can have some, too, if she brushes her teeth again afterward."

"Thanks," I said.

Of course, once her mother was gone, Carly stopped screaming. Kids always stop, so I hadn't been worried. But I did think she looked a little flushed. Perhaps she was coming down with the flu or something.

"Let's have some ice cream," I suggested. "Then you can pick out four books."

"Four?" asked Carly. I usually limit her to three.

"Yep. As a special treat. Four," I said, feeling sorry for her.

Honey, the dog, followed us into the kitchen and watched, wagging her tail as I served out the ice cream. "Chocolate's your favorite, isn't it?" I asked her.

Carly nodded her head.

I ate my portion and Carly ate a little of hers. Mostly, she played with the melting scoop of ice cream. Later, I realized that should have proved to me that she wasn't well.

"Are you ready for your stories?" I asked.

Carly nodded. I put her dish on the floor so that Honey, who had been waiting patiently, could lick it up. Then I walked with Carly toward the bathroom. "First you have to brush your teeth," I reminded her.

"No." She pouted.

"Don't you remember what your mother said? She said you could have ice cream if you brushed your teeth afterward."

"You're not brushing your teeth," Carly pointed out.

"I can't. My toothbrush is at home. I'll brush them later."

"I'll brush my teeth later, too," said Carly stubbornly.

I decided that one night without tooth brushing could not destroy her teeth. "All right," I agreed.

Carly picked out four books from her bookshelf and brought them over to her bed. "This one first," she said, handing me *Madeline*.

I started reading, though of course by now I know the entire text by heart. Carly leaned against me, breathing heavily. Perhaps if I had been reading any other book except *Madeline*, I would just have concentrated on the words and not started thinking. But knowing the text from memory, I could let my mind

wander. And because the story told of a little girl with an attack of appendicitis, I began to wonder if Carly might have something serious like that wrong with her.

"Does anything hurt you?" I asked, interrupting my reading.

Carly nodded.

"Where? Is it your stomach?" I asked anxiously.

"Everywhere," said Carly, sniffling.

I leaned over and touched my lips to her forehead. It was the way my mother always tested if I was running a fever when I was Carly's age. It seemed to me that her head felt warm. Could she have gotten a fever since I arrived?

I became scared. If Carly was sick, what should I do? "Wait here a minute," I said to her. I went into the bathroom and got her washcloth from the towel rack over the tub. I ran cold water on it and then squeezed it out. Back in Carly's room, I wiped her face with the cool cloth.

"Does that feel good?" I asked her. I remembered my mother doing that to me.

Carly nodded. She was lying back in her bed, with her eyes half-closed. What else could I do to make her feel better?

"Now I'm going to get you a cool drink," I said. My mother always makes me drink a lot of liquids when I am ill.

I wished that Mr. and Mrs. Rustin had gone to visit friends that evening. Then they would have left me a phone number to call them. How could I reach them at a movie theater? I didn't even know which theater they had gone to.

At that moment, I felt just like Ellie. I hated baby-sitting. I wished I was at home, curled up with a good book or playing Scrabble with my parents. Anything would be better than being alone in the Rustins' home, with Carly running a temperature in her bed-room.

On the Rustins' refrigerator, Carly's mother had left a list of numbers. I found the pediatrician's num-ber and dialed it. Carly is probably only coming down with a cold or something, I told myself, hoping I was right. Maybe the doctor would be annoyed that I was bothering him on a Saturday evening. But why did Mrs. Rustin leave that number for me if she didn't ex-pect me to use it?

Of course, at 8:30 on a Saturday evening, I didn't reach the doctor. I got his answering service. "Tell him that Carly Rustin has a temperature," I said. It sounded pretty dumb when I said that. Everyone has a temperature. Even healthy people have a tempera-ture—98.6. "I mean a fever. I'm the baby-sitter and I'm not sure what's wrong with her."

"What is her temperature?" the woman on the other end of the line inquired after she had asked me for the Rustins' telephone number.

"I don't know. I didn't actually take it. But she feels hot."

"How old is the child?" the woman asked.

"Three."

"You could give her a baby aspirin," she said. "I'll have the doctor call you back as soon as I can reach him."

I felt a little better having spoken to the woman, but while the phone was still in my hand, I decided to call my mother. She'd be able to tell me what to do. The phone at home rang and rang, and at about the seventh ring, I remembered that my parents had been invited out to dinner. Just as I was about to hang up the phone, I heard a voice.

"Hello." It was Stephen.

"Oh, Stephen." I sighed with relief. He knew so much. He was just as good a person to talk to as my mother. "I'm so glad you're home. I'm baby-sitting over at the Rustins' and little Carly is burning up with a fever."

"Did you give her anything?" Stephen asked.

"I'm going to give her an aspirin in a minute. I called the doctor, too. He's going to call me back."

"Well, then, stop worrying. That's all you can do for now," he said.

"Couldn't you come over here and keep me company?" I begged. "I'm scared."

"Don't be silly, Sunny," he said. "Nancy and I are watching a video. We could stop it and come over, but what good would that do? Go give Carly her aspirin and relax. You're a wonderful baby-sitter and Carly's lucky to have you taking care of her."

"Please, Stephen," I begged again.

"Listen, you should hang up," said Stephen. "Otherwise, if the doctor tries to phone, he won't be able to reach you."

"Oh. Right. I didn't think of that," I said. "Okay. Bye, Stephen."

"Bye, and stop worrying," were Stephen's last words as he hung up.

I went to the medicine cabinet and found a little bottle of baby aspirin. They were just like the type Stephen and I had taken when we were little—orange-flavored. I read the instructions on the bottle. Carly was big enough to take two of them. I hoped she liked them as much as I had. Then I read the rest of the instructions. *Do not give in cases of flu or chicken pox.* Help. How was I supposed to know what was wrong?

I returned to Carly without the aspirins. She was half-asleep. "Drink this," I said, shaking her awake and giving her a glass of apple juice.

She swallowed a little of the juice. "You didn't finish my story," she reminded me in a sleepy voice.

So I sat on her bed, reading to the end of the book even though she fell asleep before I concluded.

I sat next to Carly and listened to her breathing. When I put my lips to her forehead, I really couldn't tell if she felt cooler or hotter. I wanted her to be cooler so much that I kept telling myself that she was, but I was very scared. I wished the doctor would phone. I wished Mr. and Mrs. Rustin would come home. I wished Stephen had come to keep me company. I wished my mother was home. I'd been baby-sitting for more than two years, but this was the first time a child had ever gotten ill when I was baby-sitting. I felt absolutely helpless. I didn't want anything bad to happen to Carly.

The telephone rang and I jumped with a start. I rushed out of the room to answer it.

"Dr. Simmons here," said a cheery voice.

"Oh, Dr. Simmons. I'm baby-sitting with Carly Rustin. And she's burning hot. I wanted to give her two baby aspirin. But the directions on the bottle say not to use if a child has flu or chicken pox. I can't reach her parents. They're at a movie. I don't know what I should do." I stopped to catch my breath.

"What's Carly doing now?" asked the doctor.

"She's sleeping."

"Good. Did she throw up or complain of any pains?"

"She said she hurt everywhere, but she didn't throw up," I responded, relieved I had been spared that possibility.

"Don't be alarmed," the doctor said. "Children often run fevers, especially at night. And there's a lot of flu going around at this time of year. Tell her parents to call me in the morning if she is worse. But she'll probably be her old self within twenty-four hours. Kids are very resilient, you know."

"What about baby-sitters?" I asked. I liked the doctor's voice. He sounded so reassuring.

"Baby-sitters are very resilient, too. And they can go

home in a little while," he reminded me. "So don't worry. But you were smart to phone. It was the responsible thing to do."

Honey had been lying on the floor, sleeping, as I spoke. Suddenly, she sat up and looked toward the side door.

"Oh, wait," I said. "I think I hear Carly's parents now." I hadn't really heard them at all, but I knew that Honey could recognize the sound of their car's engine. She always greeted them at the door when they returned at night.

Sure enough, a moment later, the door opened. I was even more relieved to see the Rustins than I had been the week before to see Curtis Silvers.

"Carly's got a fever," I said quickly, and handed the phone to Mrs. Rustin. "I called your pediatrician."

"Dr. Simmons, hello," Mrs. Rustin said.

"My wife was worried that she might be coming down with something," Carly's father said, taking me aside. "That's why we didn't even stop somewhere for a cup of coffee. We wanted to get back quickly." He went to look at his daughter.

Mrs. Rustin hung up the phone and went to look at Carly, too.

"I don't think she has much of a fever," Mrs. Rustin said a moment later when she returned to the living room. "She's sound asleep."

"I'm glad you're back," I said. "It's scary to see a child get sick."

"Taking care of a child is the biggest challenge in

the world," Mrs. Rustin said. "No one ever explained to me that being a parent is a twenty-four-hour-a-day job. But it's got lots of rewards, too."

"Here's *your* reward," said Mr. Rustin, opening his wallet.

"Hey, that's too much," I protested. "You weren't gone that long."

"It's what they call combat pay, a bonus that you earn when you're in a dangerous situation," he said. "Carly wasn't really in any danger and neither were you. But it's great for my wife and me to know that we have someone like you we can trust taking care of our daughter."

"I looked for you at the dance last week," Mrs. Rustin said, "but it was so crowded, I didn't see you. I'm afraid that before I know it, I'm going to lose my best baby-sitter."

"Don't worry," I told her. "It looks like my weekends are going to be free for years to come." I didn't tell her the horror story of that Saturday night.

"You're still young," said Mrs. Rustin. "Before you know it, you're going to have a very, very busy social life."

I smiled and shrugged my shoulders as I followed Mr. Rustin out to the car so he could drive me home. I remembered the words my grandmother used to say when someone made a prediction that she liked: "From your lips to God's ears."

# FOUR
## ❖ *The Eye Exam* ❖

I HAD AN appointment to get my eyes examined on the second Saturday morning in March. It was now two weeks since that Leap Year Dance. Not one day had passed since then that I hadn't hoped that Curtis would call me. He hadn't. Perhaps he never would.

As my mother and I were getting ready to leave the house, Stephen looked up from the English muffin on which he was spreading strawberry jam. "Don't forget, the letters on the bottom line are *K-R-S-C-T-B-O-M*," he told me. "And don't worry if you can't remember," he added. "Nobody's perfect!"

I grinned. If anyone in the world had memorized the bottom line of an eye chart, it would be Stephen. But on the other hand, he could have been joking, too. It didn't really matter. Within seconds, I couldn't recall the sequence of letters he had recited. Was it *K-B-S-T-O...*? I didn't know. And it wouldn't do me any good to try and fudge the reading anyhow. I really can't see without glasses. That's the true bottom line!

If you have to wear glasses every day of your life, the way I do, you'll understand how I look forward to the time every couple of years when my mom announces that I can select new frames. But new frames are expensive, and unfortunately for me, this was not one of those years when I would be buying new ones.

At the vision center, my mom pulled her library book from her oversized tote bag. "You don't need me to go in with you," she said. It was a statement, not a question.

"Of course not," I responded. "I'm a big girl now."

"Good. This mystery is just getting exciting," she said.

So ten minutes later, I was on my own when the receptionist called my name. She showed me into a little cubicle and told me the doctor would be with me in a moment. When he came in, he wasn't either of the two who had examined my eyes in the past. He was new. Also young and very good-looking. I could tell that even with my glasses off.

"Hello, Allison," he greeted me. "I'm Dr. Gregory."

"Hi," I mumbled, as I played with my glasses. The doctor began flashing lights in my eyes. Next, he tested me with the funny machine that makes circles get bigger and brighter when you try to focus. "You've got beautiful eyes," he complimented me. "They are a great color—not blue and not green. Something between the two."

"Yeah, but no one can really appreciate the color when I'm wearing my glasses," I complained to him.

"Did you ever think of getting contacts?" he asked.

"Of course," I said. "Doesn't everyone who wears glasses think about contact lenses?"

He turned to some drawers at the side of the room

and shuffled through the various supplies inside. "Hold still," he instructed.

I felt something in my left eye for a fraction of a second, and then when I blinked, I didn't feel anything at all.

Dr. Gregory focused on my right eye and I felt the same sensation I had felt a moment before. But again, when I blinked, all was fine.

"Take a look," the doctor said to me, handing me a mirror. "What do you see?"

I stared in the mirror. "I see me," I said. Who else was I supposed to see?

"Can you see clearly? Can you read the words on that picture?" he asked, pointing to a framed cartoon that was hanging on the wall.

" 'I don't care if I can't read the little numbers. I don't think I'd like to know'?" I read. There was a picture of a very fat man standing on a bathroom scale.

"So what do you think?" asked Dr. Gregory.

"What did you do?" I asked, suddenly realizing that I was reading without wearing glasses for the first time in almost ten years.

"What do you think I did?" he asked. He was a big one for asking questions instead of giving answers, I noticed.

I looked at myself again in the mirror. My blue-green eyes shone at me with a clarity and a brilliance I had never seen before. They really and truly looked beautiful. I could hardly believe they were mine.

"Did you put contact lenses in my eyes?" I asked incredulously.

Dr. Gregory nodded his head. "So what do you think?" he asked again. "The price of lenses has gone way down in the last few years. It's no more than for a pair of good eyeglasses these days. And I think you'll find that you'll actually see better with the lenses than with glasses. And they certainly enhance your looks."

"I love them," I said. "I just love them." I felt as if I were another person, as if I'd just had a fairy godmother wave her wand and transform me from an ugly duckling into a swan. I know I'm confusing those old fairy tales, but that's the way I felt. "I always thought contacts would hurt," I confessed to the doctor. "You know, it hurts so much when you get an eyelash or a speck of dirt in your eye. But I can't feel anything. It's like magic."

"I knew you'd be pleased with the results. So many people are afraid of trying something new. So sometimes I just put the lenses in a patient's eyes. It convinces them every time. You just have to remember two things: Don't wear them when you are sleeping, or you'll irritate your eyes. And don't cry when you wear them, or you'll wash them out."

"I'm convinced!" I said, as I jumped off the examining chair. "I may never go to sleep again," I added, laughing. "And I've nothing in the world to cry about, either. Wait till I show my mother. She'll be as surprised as I was."

I charged out of the examining room and rushed into the waiting area, where my mother was deeply engrossed in her book. "Mom. Look at me. What do you see?" I asked her, unconsciously adopting the style of Dr. Gregory.

My mother looked up, startled. Then she smiled at me. "I see my daughter, who just had her eyes examined," she said. "And now let's go somewhere where I can have a cup of coffee. You can have hot chocolate."

"Look at me some more," I instructed her. "There's a mystery right in front of you, as well as in the book you are reading."

"A mystery? What are you talking about, Sunny?" she asked in a puzzled voice.

"Don't you notice anything strange about me? What kind of a detective would you make?" I teased her.

"Strange? Well, you're not wearing your glasses, if that's what you mean," she answered.

"Right," I said, practically jumping up and down in front of her and all the other people in the waiting room. "And why am I not wearing my glasses?"

"Did you leave them in the examining room?" she asked.

"Oh, Mom, you're so slow. You'd never make a detective," I said, hugging her. "I'm wearing contact lenses. Isn't it wonderful? I can see perfectly. They don't hurt, and I love the way I look."

By now, everyone in the waiting area was looking at me. I felt like a walking advertisement for contact lenses. It was wonderful!

"Sunny. What do you mean, you're wearing contact lenses? I didn't say you could buy them."

"I know, but the price is almost the same as for

glasses. Dr. Gregory explained it to me. He put the lenses in my eyes in a second and without my even knowing it. That just shows how easy they are to insert. And I can't feel a thing. I just love them," I said again.

"Well, that's too bad, honey. I told you that I didn't budget for new frames. Next year, when you're fifteen, we'll talk about it."

"Next year?" I cried out. Next year, Curtis Silvers would be off at college. There was no one else at the high school I wanted to attract. "What about my babysitting money?" I offered. Then I remembered the two new sweaters I had splurged on. Why had I bought them? I was almost broke.

"It's not only money," my mother admitted then. "I really worry that fourteen is too young for contacts. I've read a couple of articles on the subject of lenses. Some doctors feel that it's better to wait until you're a bit older—when your vision has stabilized. The doctor here had no right to put them into your eyes without first consulting me. I'm sorry to disappoint you, honey, but we're going right back into the office and he's going to remove them at once."

If the waiting area hadn't been so full of patients, I know I would have let out a terrible cry of anger and disappointment. I had never wanted anything as much as I wanted those contact lenses. But I just couldn't make a scene at the vision center. Besides, I remembered that Dr. Gregory had warned me not to cry when I was wearing the lenses.

So I sniffed back my tears and tried in vain to think

of an argument that would change my mother's mind. If only Stephen was with us. He'd have known what to say.

My mother accompanied me back to the examining cubicle and we waited for Dr. Gregory to return.

"How do you do," he said, putting out his hand. "I take it you are Allison's mother. Doesn't she look stunning without her glasses?"

"To me, my daughter always looks stunning," my mother said sharply. "Wearing glasses is not a detraction, because beauty is inside a person, not merely on the outside. You really shouldn't have put lenses in her eyes without the permission of her parents. It wasn't right."

I sat in the examining chair and blushed with embarrassment for Dr. Gregory. My mom was talking to him just as if he were one of her fourth graders.

Dr. Gregory turned red and suddenly looked a lot younger, almost like a boy who had gotten into mischief.

"But, Mrs. Marx, Allison isn't a child. Shouldn't she be permitted to make some decisions about her own appearance? The lenses aren't just cosmetic. They actually do improve her vision."

"Have you read her chart?" my mother asked. "Do you know how old she is?"

Dr. Gregory turned his head, looking for the chart with the information about me. It was across the room, and no matter how good his eyes were, he couldn't read the fine print from where he was standing.

He turned back to me and said, "I imagine she must be seventeen or eighteen."

For a moment, I forgot how upset I was, because I was so flattered by the doctor's words.

"She's only fourteen," my mother said, and suddenly I felt like a little kid again.

"Fourteen?" he asked. "I really thought she was older."

"Now please remove those lenses from her eyes," my mother said, softly but firmly. "I've promised Sunny that we'll talk about lenses in the future. But not today."

At that point, I could not suppress the sob that escaped from me.

Afterward, my mother offered to take me out to lunch as a distraction. I didn't want to go.

"Just take me home," I said, feeling very sorry for myself.

"Sunny. Someday when you are a mother, you'll understand. What your children want is not always possible or even the best for them," she said as we were driving home.

"But I looked so beautiful without my glasses. I was like a different person," I tried to explain to her.

"Sunny, I wish I could make you realize how lovely you look, just as you are. I could hardly believe how great you looked on the evening of the school dance when you were all dressed up." She took one hand off the wheel and reached out and squeezed one of mine. "I guess I shouldn't remind you of that dance, but there will be a hundred others and a hundred other dates coming your way."

"Tell that to Curtis Silvers," I mumbled, half to myself and half to her. I felt pretty certain that no one would ever call me for Saturday night except a mother looking for a baby-sitter.

# FIVE
## ❧ *Mirabile Dictu* ❧

NOW HERE'S THE most amazing thing: The very next morning, around eleven o'clock, I went to the phone to call Ellie. I wanted to check with her about an assignment we had for social studies. Just as my hand was about to lift the telephone receiver, it rang. So I picked it up in the middle of the first ring.

"Hello?" I said.

There was a slight pause and then a husky, unfamiliar voice on the other end said, "Uh, hello. Uh. Is this Sunny? This is Curtis Silvers."

"Oh," I gasped with surprise. I'd never heard Curtis's voice on the phone, so I hadn't recognized it. In fact, I'd hardly ever heard his voice anywhere. "Do you want to talk to Stephen?"

As soon as I said it, I thought how stupid I was. Of course he was calling to speak with my brother. But I realized I should have tried to make a little conversation with him first.

"Uh, no. Uh. I'm calling to see if you want to go out with me next Friday night. There's a new Steven Spielberg film opening. I think it'll be good."

I didn't care if it was good or not. "Sure," I said eagerly. My face grew hot and my heart was beating rapidly. "I'd love to go."

"Okay. I'll come by your house around seven

o'clock. We should get there early because there'll probably be a long line."

"Okay," I answered. I almost said, Don't go for any drives with your cousin, but luckily I didn't. I would have meant it as a joke, but maybe he wouldn't have taken it that way.

Curtis hung up and I stood holding the phone and smiling at it. I remembered a phrase that Stephen had learned in his Latin class: "mirabile dictu." It means "wonderful to say," and after he learned that phrase, Stephen used to walk into the house and say, "Mirabile dictu, I've been made one of the starters for the basketball team." Or, "Mirabile dictu, my teacher gave me an *A*-plus on that report I did for English." Most recently, it was, "Mirabile dictu, I got into Harvard!"

In all my life, I'd rarely had occasion to say "mirabile dictu." Now I felt like shouting those words out loud.

I immediately dialed Ellie's number. I had to share my news with her at once. I got her mother. "How are you, Sunny?" she asked.

"I'm just fine," I responded, beaming at the wall in front of me.

"I'll get Ellie, but don't stay on the phone long, okay? I'm expecting a call from my sister. We take turns calling each other on Sunday mornings," she explained.

"Sure." I smiled at the wall.

Ellie got on the phone. "Hi, what's up?" she asked.

"Mirabile dictu, he called and asked me for a date."

"What?" Ellie asked, puzzled. She doesn't take Latin.

"Mirabile dictu. It means 'wonderful to say.' Curtis Silvers just phoned here, and he's taking me to the movies next Friday night," I almost shouted into the phone.

"Well, that's the least he could do after the mess he made the night of the dance," said Ellie.

"It wasn't his fault," I said, defending him. "And anyhow, it shows he wants to see me again."

"Again? He hardly saw you at all," said Ellie.

"Don't be mean. If I'm not angry at him, why are you?" I asked her.

"Because I'm your friend," she reminded me.

"In that case, ask me when he called and what he said," I instructed her. I was dying to tell the whole story over and over. It was like a dream, but by repeating it a few times, I'd get to believe that it was true.

"When did he call and what did he say?" asked Ellie, giggling.

So I repeated my conversation with Curtis from beginning to end. It wasn't a long conversation, so I told her everything twice.

"Well, it sounds great," she said. "But my mother is glaring at me. I've got to get off the phone. I'll see you tomorrow. Maybe there'll be something new for you to report. Sunny Silvers has a great ring to it," she added as she hung up.

"Sunny Silvers," I whispered to myself. It did sound good.

I ran to tell my family the news. Stephen grinned. "I hope this date works out better than the last," he said. He sounded a little like Ellie.

It wasn't until the middle of the afternoon, when I was sitting down to do my homework, that I realized I'd never asked Ellie anything about the social studies assignment.

I could hardly wait till Friday, and I figured out what I'd wear about six different times. A movie on a Friday evening was a casual sort of date, so I knew I should wear pants. But should I wear jeans or woolen slacks? Should I wear a shirt or a sweater?

Ellie and I discussed my entire wardrobe over lunch each day, and by Friday evening when Curtis rang my doorbell, I was wearing my newest jeans with a turtleneck cotton sweater and a scarf. Casual, but fancy casual.

"Uh, hi," said Curtis.

"Uh, hi," I responded.

He was wearing jeans, too, and, unlike two weeks before when he'd come to my house, there was no dirt or grease on his face or hands. He was chewing a piece of gum.

I grabbed my jacket and put it on. I remembered how Mr. Rustin had helped his wife put her coat on. Oh, well. One can't expect everything.

The movie theater was a few blocks away. We started off and I waited for Curtis to say something. I guess he was waiting for me to say something. Neither of us spoke. I watched my breath turn to steam as I exhaled into the cold evening air. Being so tall, Curtis has long legs. He walked quickly and I had to move fast to keep up with his pace. "I'm glad it's not raining," I said. Boy, was I stupid. All I could talk about was the weather.

"Yeah. Right," Curtis agreed.

We walked on in silence. Curtis snapped his gum from time to time. That, plus the noise our shoes made hitting the sidewalk as we walked, were the only sounds we made. A few cars went by along the street. I saw an elderly man walking his dog. But nothing gave me an idea of something to talk about. I guess nothing gave Curtis an idea of something to talk about, either.

"I heard this is a great picture," I said finally. "It got great reviews in the paper."

"Yeah," Curtis agreed.

"Did you see his last film?" I asked.

"Yeah," said Curtis. His gum snapped in his mouth. "I go to all the Spielberg movies."

I wondered who had gone with him last time.

Although we were forty-five minutes early, there was already a line forming in front of the movie house. "Wait here," said Curtis. "I'll get the tickets."

I stood on line and looked to see if I recognized anyone ahead of me. There was a girl from my math class. She was with a couple of girls I didn't know. I also saw our neighbors the Hendersons. They saw me and waved. Too bad they didn't see me standing next to my handsome date. I sighed. They probably thought I'd come alone.

I watched for Curtis. I saw him holding the tickets and talking with a couple of guys near the front of the line. I didn't know their names, but I recognized them from school. Finally, Curtis returned. By then, there were a lot of people standing behind me.

"It's good we got here early," I said.

"Uh, yeah," Curtis agreed. He snapped his gum. "The line is really long."

I looked at his handsome face. I could tell he had shaved recently. There was a tiny drop of dried blood on his chin. I guess, with his dark hair, he had to shave more often than Stephen, who is blond. Maybe Curtis has to shave every day, I thought, impressed.

Curtis looked at me and I looked away. What could I say to him? "The basketball team is doing really great this season," I said.

"Uh, yeah. Your brother is the greatest," he said.

"You're pretty good, too," I complimented him.

"Uh, thanks." He chewed his gum. "We have a great coach," he added as an afterthought.

I nodded in agreement and sighed to myself. This is really hard work, I thought. Who would have believed that conversation with Curtis Silvers would be harder than algebra? All around me, people were talking to one another. How come they could think of things to say? A cold wind blew, and I shivered under my down jacket.

"It's cold," I said. Oh, dear. I was talking about the weather again.

The line began to inch forward. At least when we

were sitting in our seats, watching the film, I wouldn't have to worry about making conversation. The effort was really wearing me out.

"I like an aisle seat," Curtis shouted as we pushed our way into the door and were temporarily separated by about a hundred other people. I kept my eyes on Curtis, and he charged toward a pair of seats on the aisle.

"I guess with your height, you must feel cramped when you go to the movies," I said, sitting down. "My legs are pretty long, too. For a girl, I mean. But usually, I get so engrossed in whatever picture I'm watching, I forget about them. Sometimes at the end of the film, I discover they've fallen asleep and I didn't even know."

"Uh, yeah," said Curtis. "Do you like popcorn?"

Should I say yes? Should I offer to pay? After all, he had paid for the tickets. Curtis snapped his gum. That gum was driving me crazy. If we had popcorn, he'd have to spit the gum out. "I love popcorn," I said.

"Save the seat," said Curtis, and he was gone.

I watched as the seats around me filled up. There were many faces from school that I half-recognized in the semidarkness.

Curtis returned with a giant-sized container of popcorn. It was almost the size of a wastepaper basket. Obviously, he liked popcorn, too. "Help yourself," he said, sitting down and putting the container in his lap.

The theater darkened and the coming attractions began. I put my hand into the container of popcorn and touched one of Curtis's fingers. Ah, I thought. This is more like it. This was a detail that I could share with Ellie.

I was so aware of sitting next to handsome Curtis Silvers that it took me awhile to get into the film. Every time I reached for some popcorn, there was the possibility that his hand would be in the container, too.

Curtis seemed immediately engrossed. He chewed away on the popcorn and kept his eyes on the screen. Eventually, I also got under the movie's spell. Of course, there were a few tense moments in the film. In my family, everyone knows that during moments of suspense, I need to hold someone's hand. When we watch a scary film on TV or a video, one of my parents or Stephen holds out a hand for me. I didn't want to be forward, but I needed Curtis's hand in the worst way. He was still shoveling the popcorn into his mouth. Finally, I just closed my eyes and held my own hand. I know it sounds stupid, but what could I do?

When the film was over, I thought we'd probably go to the Finer Diner for a snack. That's where Stephen usually stops with his dates. It's an enormous place, and it's open twenty-four hours a day. Whatever hour you walk in there, you'll find people eating. Some will be in the middle of huge meals, but you can also just order a sandwich or a slice of pie. I've eaten in the diner with my parents, and a couple of times Stephen has taken me there for dessert after a film. Almost always, we find other people he knows. I was looking

forward to entering with Curtis and sitting together with a group of other high school kids. I wanted to show off that I was with Curtis.

I was dying of thirst from the popcorn. But we didn't go toward the diner, where I could get something to drink. I walked along with Curtis, wondering if he knew of some other place. "What did you think of the film?" I asked.

"Okay," he said, snapping again on a piece of gum. Is it the same piece as before? I wondered. I didn't see him put it in his mouth.

I was out of breath from keeping up with Curtis's pace when we reached my front door. Obviously, Curtis wasn't planning on taking me out after the movie. But maybe he doesn't have any more money, I thought.

"Come in and I'll make some hot chocolate," I offered.

"Uh, no thanks," said Curtis.

"You could have tea or coffee or milk instead," I added.

"Uh, uh, no thanks," said Curtis.

"Well, thanks for taking me to the film," I said. "I really enjoyed it. It was fun to spend the evening with you."

"Yeah. Well, my mother sort of hinted that I owed it to you. That was a mess the night of the dance, wasn't it?" He shrugged his shoulders. "Well. Uh, so long." And he turned and walked off, his long legs taking him quickly away down my street.

I stood speechless. I'd been speechless most of the evening. But now I knew it wasn't that I was such a social dud. Curtis Silvers had taken me out because his mother said he had to. Not because he liked me. Not because he wanted to get to know me better. Not because he was sorry about standing me up the evening of the dance.

Curtis Silvers might be one of the handsomest guys in Hoover High School, but he sure didn't have any social graces. He didn't even know enough to pretend to be friendly. What good were his looks if he couldn't find anything to say? It was like going out on a date with a cardboard statue of some movie star. It might look impressive from a distance, but close up it was as boring as could be.

I opened the door and went in. Luckily, no one was home to ask me about the evening. I got ready for bed and realized something. Mirabile dictu, my infatuation with Curtis Silvers was over!

# SIX
## ❧ *Mom's Birthday* ❧

THURSDAY, MARCH 19, was my mother's fortieth birthday. I suggested to Stephen that we throw a surprise birthday party for her the weekend before or after the big day. But when we discussed it with Dad, he said it wasn't such a great idea.

"Parties are swell," he said, "but your mother isn't exactly thrilled to be so old. She certainly won't want to celebrate it with a party."

"It's better than the alternative," Stephen pointed out.

"Of course." Dad smiled. "But she doesn't want to be reminded that she is entering her fifth decade."

"Fifth decade?" I asked, puzzled. Math, as you know, isn't my strong point, so it took me a moment to figure out what he meant. "When you put it that way, it sounds ancient," I said when I understood. I could sympathize with how my mother felt. What did she have to look forward to? Old age? I may have days when being fourteen is difficult, but I certainly wouldn't want to be forty. At least there was so much I could look ahead to—college, marriage, a career, children…. But she had done it all already. And now she was forty and still in fourth grade.

"So what are you going to do? Will you take her out to dinner?" I asked.

"That was my plan. Just a quiet, romantic evening out for the two of us. But guess what? She wants both of you kids to come along."

"That's not very romantic." Stephen laughed.

"It won't be quiet, either," I added.

"I agree," my father said. "But she says this is the last year we'll all be together. Next year at this time, Stephen will be off in college."

"If she misses me that much, I'll come home for her birthday," offered Stephen.

"It's not a matter of coming home for a weekend or an event. This is a turning point in all our lives. So she wants to have us all together before we move on to the next phase."

"You won't exactly have an empty nest," I reminded him. "I'm going to be around for another three years."

"Good," Dad said, giving me a hug. "Take your time."

"The way she's doing in algebra, she is," Stephen pointed out.

"No fair," I objected. "You know I passed the last two exams."

"Thanks to me," Stephen said, putting his arm around me. The gesture softened his words.

"Someday I'll help you with something," I promised. "Just be patient."

"What?" asked Stephen.

It was a good question, and I didn't have an answer. I couldn't imagine independent, clever Stephen ever needing my help for anything.

"She could sew that button on your sweater," Dad commented, pointing to a pewter button that was hanging by a single thread.

"That's a great idea," said Stephen, starting to take off his sweater.

"No it isn't. It's sexist to think that I can sew your button because I'm a female. Sew it yourself. It's good practice for when you go away to school and Mom and I aren't around to do things for you."

"I can do it, but you said you would help me out one of these days," said Stephen.

"I will," I promised him, "and it will be something more important than a button."

Since it was Mom's birthday, she chose where we would eat. She picked La Grande Cuisine, which is a French restaurant in the next town. Dad made the reservation for 7:00 P.M., but at 7:00 A.M. as he was eating breakfast and reading the newspaper that Thursday morning, he saw a small notice that a kitchen fire had closed the restaurant the evening before.

"Oh, dear," Mom joked. "Do you think it's an omen? Now that I'm forty, only bad things are going to happen."

"The fire was a bad thing for La Grande Cuisine, not you," Stephen pointed out. He handed Mom the box with the gift we were giving her jointly. Inside was a silk scarf, which I had picked out and we had ordered from a catalog of the Metropolitan Museum of Art in New York City. It was expensive, and it was beautiful. I knew Mom would like it. And she did.

"Oh, this is fantastic," she said as she removed the scarf from its tissue paper and opened it up to admire it all. It was a reproduction of a mosaic floor somewhere in Israel, in shades of brown and tan and blue.

Dad gave Mom a bracelet. She wore it and her new scarf when we went out that evening. When Dad had phoned from his office to the only other elegant restaurant in our area to make an alternate reservation, they could only seat us at 9:00 P.M.—too late, we all agreed, for dinner. Three of us had to get up for school the next morning. And Dad had to be in court for a case he was handling.

Mom had come home from work with a huge arrangement of spring flowers from her class. Somehow, someone had heard it was her birthday, and the children and their parents had thrown a surprise party in her classroom and given the flowers.

She was so delighted with the unexpected celebration in her class that I poked Stephen and said, "We should have thrown her a party. She would have liked it after all."

He shrugged his shoulders. "There's no law that says you can't make a surprise party for someone when they turn forty-one. In fact, if you do that, everyone will probably think it's a party for her fortieth birthday. You'll make her a year younger. She'll like that."

"Good idea," I agreed, and made a mental note to start planning for next year.

Instead of elegance, we were going to a new Chinese restaurant that had opened nearby. We all like Chinese food, so it wasn't a hardship, even if the evening wasn't quite as originally planned.

"We can go another evening to La Grande Cuisine," Dad promised.

So there we were, surrounded by chicken and cashews, beef and broccoli, brown rice, eggplant with garlic sauce, and goodness knows what else.

Mom and Dad were eating with forks, but Stephen was using chopsticks. I'm not sure where and when he mastered them, but there's nothing Stephen can't master, as we all know very well.

"Hold them like this." He showed me. I tried to copy him. It looked like fun.

Suddenly, in the midst of our meal, a heavyset dark-haired man sitting nearby banged his hand down hard on his table. We looked over at him, expecting that he was making a point in an argument or something. Instead, he made a gasping sound and his face turned a bright red color.

The man's dinner companions all sat staring at him as the man hit the table again and again.

"What's wrong?" Mom asked. She grabbed Dad's hand.

I stopped chewing my mouthful of food and just stared.

"He's choking!" exclaimed Stephen.

We all watched in a trance as one of the waiters threw down the tray he was carrying and rushed to the man's aid. He pulled the man out of his chair. Then, using both arms, he grabbed him from the back and locked his arms under the man's jacket and around the area above his stomach.

"It's the Heimlich maneuver," Dad said.

Finally, after a second or two, the waiter exerted the proper pressure, which released the object caught in the man's windpipe. A piece of half-chewed meat was dislodged and came flying out of the man's mouth.

The other waiters and all the diners burst into applause as the natural color returned to the man's face. Stephen turned to us, as flushed as if he had been the one who had exerted the pressure on the man. "Wasn't that something?" he marveled.

The man took a drink of water and shook his head with disbelief. "I've read about it happening, but I never thought it could happen to me," he said in a hoarse voice.

"It can happen to anyone, anytime," said Stephen. "I took a CPR course a few weeks ago, and they spent about fifteen minutes on what to do if someone chokes while eating. I knew it was an important technique to learn, but I didn't expect to see a live demonstration while I was having dinner tonight."

"Oh, wasn't that ghastly," my mother commented. "He could have died right in front of us."

"But he didn't. Thank God for that," my father said.

I realized that I still had food in my mouth. I had stopped chewing during the moments it had taken to save the man. Now, I was afraid to swallow, and so I spit into my napkin.

None of us had any appetite to finish our meal after what we had witnessed.

"Do you think it's an omen?" my mother asked as we got ready to leave the restaurant. It was the second time that day she asked that question.

"Don't be silly," Dad said. "Everyone's fine now."

The waiter packed up our food in those little white containers they have in Chinese restaurants. I couldn't imagine having an appetite to eat that food the next day. I wasn't sure I could eat Chinese food for a long, long time, with or without chopsticks.

With all those food boxes, our car smelled like a Chinese restaurant on the way home. "I think that man choking *was* an omen," my mother said, obsessed with looking for messages in everything that had happened that day.

"I may be forty, but at least I'm alive and well. I have two wonderful children and a great husband. I have a job I love...." She couldn't go on, because she was crying.

Dad pulled the car over to the side of the road. "Susan," he said. "I've been telling you, there are a lot of things in the world worse than turning forty."

Mom reached in her purse for a tissue. "You're right," she said. "It could have been one of us who choked. One could die from one minute to the next. You never think about that, but it's true. So we should just enjoy each other and our lives and..." Again, she broke off into tears.

"Oh, Mom," Stephen protested. "Don't be so morbid. If you start choking, I can save you. You don't have to worry, with me around. I just wish I'd been the one to do it tonight. What a great feeling it must be to save someone's life. I really wish I had moved faster," he said, sounding annoyed with himself for missing the chance.

It seemed like a strange way for him to react to such a terrible scene. There were the rest of us, and probably all the other diners at the restaurant as well, wishing the events of the evening had never occurred, and at the same time, Stephen was disappointed because he hadn't been the hero of the evening.

I looked at Stephen's face in the dim light and thought that he was being greedy with life. He certainly had enough accomplishments for someone his age. Now he wanted to top himself and play God. I suppose next summer at the beach, he'd try walking on water. Well, why not? If anyone could do it, it would probably be Stephen.

# SEVEN
## ❧ *Basketball Practice* ❧

ON DAYS WHEN I don't have any after-school activity, I often stop at the gym and watch my brother and his teammates at basketball practice. Of course I'm proud of Stephen. And it gives me a chance to keep an eye on Curtis. Curtis still looks great running around in his gym shorts and shaking his dark hair out of his eyes, but now I notice that his jaw works as fast as his feet. How come I never noticed that there is always a piece of gum in his mouth? And how could I have known that going out with him would be as boring as dating a tree?

Teddy Rustin is the coach of the basketball team. He has the guys practice several times a week. He's one of the most popular teachers in the school. Everyone loves him. He's got a great sense of humor and loads of patience. He doesn't scream at the players or make them feel bad when they lose a game.

"I know you lost the ball," he comforts them. "Next time you'll do better."

And the amazing thing, according to Stephen, is that they *do* do better the next time. The old coach who retired the year Stephen was a freshman had a different style. "Idiot! You're an idiot," he always shouted to the player who muffed a shot or dropped the ball or committed a foul.

His name was Charlie Wilson, but he used the word *idiot* so often that his team secretly referred to him as "Idiot Wilson." Stephen said it was their way of feeling better about being insulted by him all the time.

Teddy Rustin was certainly just the opposite of the old coach. He always smiled and greeted you in the hallway, even if you weren't one of his students and he didn't know your name. Of course, Teddy Rustin knew me. First, he knew me because I'm Stephen's sister and Stephen was one of his star players. And then I became his daughter's baby-sitter as well.

Some days, Mrs. Rustin and Carly come to watch during practice, too. I sit next to them and explain the rules to Carly. She can't remember them, but she pretends that she does. "Do you have something for me, Sunny?" she'll ask me. And I do. I'm probably the only girl in the high school who buys lollipops by the bag. I always carry a couple in my backpack in case I see Carly.

On the second Wednesday in April, the gym was packed during practice. Our team had made it to the county finals, and now there was just one more basketball game between us and the championship. The entire school was excited about the event and hopeful our team would go on to become the statewide high school champs.

Tickets for the big game had been sold-out for days, and everyone wanted this last chance to watch the Hoover Hoops preparing for their victory. We just knew that this was the year Hoover would win!

There must have been three hundred kids sitting in the gym that afternoon.

"Sunny. Sunny," a little voice shouted when I entered the gym. Sure enough, there was Carly with her mom. I squeezed across the bleachers till I got next to them. It was a tight fit, but I managed to make room for myself.

"Hi, Sunny. How are things?" Mrs. Rustin asked me. She was wearing her hair in a ponytail, and I thought she looked almost like a high school student herself. I had never considered how old she and her husband must be. Married people with children all seem ancient, but I guess she wasn't that old after all. And the way Teddy runs around the gym, demonstrating techniques to his players, must mean he's not so old, either.

I gave Carly her lollipop of the day. "Goody," she said. "Red is my favorite."

First, the players all did stretching exercises in time to an old ragtime tape. Stephen said that the first time Teddy Rustin announced that this was the way he wanted his guys to warm up, everyone groaned in disbelief. But by now, they're used to the idea and don't complain. It's about the funniest thing in the world to watch all those tall guys doing deep knee bends to Scott Joplin's music. We viewers in the bleachers clapped our hands to the rhythm. I saw Ellie and Mike sitting together on the other side of the gym and waved to them. They waved back.

When the music stopped, Teddy threw a bunch of basketballs to the players. They tossed them about. This was another of his tricks. With four balls going through the air, everyone had to keep looking in every direction to be sure that none of them landed on the floor. At one point, a ball was missed by Curtis, and Teddy Rustin rushed in and caught it before it hit the ground.

Then he had all the Hoops divided into a pair of teams. Everyone knew which players would be starters, but for practice he split those guys up and, together with his other players, made two teams. He blew his whistle and they started to play. As usual during practice, Teddy ran around as much as any of the team players. He was acting as coach, referee, and cheerleader all at the same time.

Suddenly, in the midst of this activity, I heard a thud. It was hard at first to see what had happened. Someone was down on the floor. I thought one of the guys had slipped and fallen. But the bodies of all the players on the gym floor blocked my view. Then I saw that it was Teddy Rustin who was lying down. Instead of jumping right up, he just lay there without moving. You could tell it was not just a twisted ankle. Something much worse had happened.

From one moment to the next, the gym became silent. The players stood frozen in place. Without Teddy, who had been telling them all year not to let themselves freeze on the court, they had all become as helpless as little kids—like Carly, whose sticky hand was in mine.

Probably only a couple of seconds passed, but it seemed much, much longer. Then Stephen pulled himself together. "Call nine-one-one," he shouted to Ben Acker, who was standing next to him. I could hear his voice all the way up in the bleachers. It sounded strained and unnatural, not like my brother's voice at all. Then Stephen got down on his hands and knees next to Teddy and started to shake him.

Of course, I knew immediately what he was doing. Hadn't he gone through all those movements on my own body? But I had only been pretending, and Teddy Rustin was not. Thank goodness Stephen took that course, I thought to myself. I squeezed Carly's hand as her mother pushed her way down to the floor of the gym to be near her husband.

Carly jumped up to follow her mother, but I held on to her.

"Mommy. Mommy," Carly called out. I didn't think she realized what was going on, but she was unprepared for her mother to rush away suddenly and leave her.

"It's okay. It's okay," I said half to myself and half to Carly, or anyone who would listen to me. If anyone could help Mr. Rustin at this moment, it was Stephen. I had total confidence in my brother's ability to help the coach at this crucial moment.

There was no pocket in Stephen's gym shorts and shirt, so he didn't have his key ring and his special mask. But he placed his mouth over the mouth of the coach and began to breathe deeply, the way he had been taught. I was so proud of him at that moment that I almost burst.

There was a low murmur of voices as people watched Stephen pumping the coach's chest and administering CPR. From where I sat, I couldn't see if the coach was breathing. All I saw was my brother's back moving, moving, moving. "Once you begin CPR," Stephen had told me, "you can never stop until a doctor comes on the scene to take over the care of the victim." I never guessed that I would have a chance to see my brother in action. And I never guessed that the victim would be someone I knew and cared about. It made this lifesaving experience even more tense than the evening in the Chinese restaurant.

It seemed like hours until the emergency ambulance arrived. But when I looked up at the clock afterward, it was only ten past four. The practice had begun at 3:45. At 3:45, we had all been listening to Scott Joplin, and less than half an hour later, I felt as if I had been sitting in the gym for a week.

Mrs. Rustin went in the ambulance with her husband. She knew Carly would be safe with me. Stephen went in the ambulance, too. I joined the hundreds of students solemnly walking out of the gym. Everyone was in a daze from the events of the afternoon, and they spoke in hushed tones together.

"I turned my head for a moment," said one guy to another. "I didn't see him fall."

"I saw him fall, but I just thought he must have slipped," his friend responded.

"Do you think he'll be okay?" someone else asked.

"Wasn't it great that Stephen Marx gave him CPR?" asked someone else.

I glowed with pride when I heard that.

"It was just like that film we saw in phys ed last month."

I held Carly's hand tightly. She had no idea what had happened.

"I'm going to take you home to my house," I told her. "You can see where I live and where I keep my lollipops."

"Do you have more red ones?" she asked.

"Maybe," I replied. I hoped I did. That was the very least I could give her that afternoon.

# EIGHT
## ❖ *A Hard Lesson* ❖

CARLY STAYED AND had supper at our house that evening. Entertaining her was one of the hardest things I've ever done. I let her comb my hair. I let her try on all my costume jewelry. I let her play with my old doll, Jennifer Anne, even though I knew the doll's head was loose and might fall off at any time. All these activities kept her busy while we waited.

Stephen came home at 6:30, and even before he opened his mouth, we knew what had happened. His pale face and expressionless eyes told it all. Mr. Rustin was dead, and Stephen had aged twenty years. He had gone into the gym that afternoon a happy-go-lucky teenager, and he had returned home looking like a middle-aged man.

"I couldn't save him," he said over and over again. "I did everything I could. But I couldn't revive him." He burst into tears and ran to his bedroom.

I was stunned. I just couldn't believe that Mr. Rustin was dead. I was sure the phone would suddenly ring. Someone would call to tell us that everything was all right after all.

My parents looked at each other helplessly. I could tell they wanted to go to Stephen, and at the same time, they understood he needed to be alone. He had to have time to himself to digest what had happened on this grim day.

When the phone did ring, it was Mrs. Rustin, who'd come back home from the hospital and was calling to check on her daughter. Dad answered, and when he hung up, I found out once and for all that it was true and not a mistake. Mr. Rustin had died.

Dad and I drove Carly home to her mother. I sat in the back with her, playing finger games and looking at her innocent face. I hadn't told her about her father. How could I? And would she even understand if I did?

Mrs. Rustin greeted us at the front door. The events of the afternoon had aged her, too. Though her hair was still pulled back, she no longer looked as young as a high school student. Her lipstick had worn off and her eyes were red. She picked Carly up and gave her a big hug.

"I played at Sunny's house," she told her mother proudly.

"Did you have a good time, sweetie?" Mrs. Rustin asked in a hoarse, strained voice.

Carly nodded her head. "Can I go to your house again tomorrow?" she demanded, turning to me.

"Sure," I said.

"Maybe not tomorrow," said Mrs. Rustin. "But soon." She tried to smile at me, but her mouth couldn't seem to make the effort.

"If there is anything we can do for you, please call," my father said. "Carly can stay at our house, even overnight, if it will make things easier for you."

"It's easier for me to have her here," said Mrs. Rustin, sighing. "But thank you for the offer."

Carly gave a yawn and started rubbing her eyes.

"Come," her mother said. "It's bedtime." She carried the little girl into the house, and the door closed behind them.

It was when the door was shut that I began crying. My father put his arm around me, and we walked to the car.

"Oh, Dad," I sobbed as we started the ride home. "It was so awful. We all saw it happen. First Mr. Rustin was running around in the gym, and then suddenly he was on the floor. It happened in a second and we all saw it. He just died in front of all of us."

"When Mrs. Rustin phoned our house before, she said her husband had had a massive heart attack," my father explained. "These things happen."

"I don't understand. Why couldn't Stephen save him? He took the CPR course. He was supposed to know what to do. He always knows what to do."

"Stephen may be first in his class and the top player on the basketball team. But that doesn't mean he can perform miracles. He could only do his best," my father said. He took his eyes off the road for a second and looked at me. "Remember that. Nobody's perfect. A person can only do their best."

I found a tissue in the pocket of my jeans and took off my glasses so I could wipe my eyes. Then I blew my nose. We pulled up in front of our house. "I guess you and all your classmates had a big lesson today," Dad said. "They can teach you literature and mathematics and social studies, but they haven't figured out a course in real life."

"What about biology?" I asked.

"Biology makes it too impersonal. It's not the same as the real thing. Watching a newborn baby is different from reading a chapter in a book about pregnancy and birth. And seeing someone die, especially if it's someone you know and care about, is a hundred percent different from reading about it in a book."

I nodded my head. He was a hundred percent right about that.

The phone was ringing when we entered the house. It must have rung dozens of times that evening. Ellie called to talk to me. Mr. Lonside, our high school principal, phoned to speak to Stephen. Then Curtis and Brian and Ben and all the other players from the basketball team called as well. But after the principal's call, Stephen locked himself in his bedroom and refused to take any others. Instead, my dad spoke to his teammates. "It's been a hard day," he told each of the guys. "Stephen's gone to bed."

Parents of some students called to speak to my parents. Everyone wanted to know the details of the afternoon. Everyone said how wonderful Stephen had been. And everyone cried on the phone. I wondered if Teddy Rustin had had any idea how beloved he was by the whole student body.

When we arrived at school the next morning,

across the entranceway there was a large white computer-paper banner with a black border. It said TEDDY RUSTIN and gave his birth and death dates. That was the first time I knew that he was thirty-seven years old. In English, we read poems about death, like "Do Not Go Gentle into That Good Night," by Dylan Thomas. The notes at the bottom of the page said that the poet had written the poem for his dying father. But that man had been a lot older than thirty-seven.

In science, we talked about heart attacks and diet. I bet it was the first day in the history of the school cafeteria that they didn't sell a single bag of potato chips or any french fries. I bet the kids who hide out and smoke in the lavatories took the day off from that activity, too.

At two o'clock, all classes were canceled, and we went to the school gym for a memorial service. We were in the gym instead of the auditorium because the gym could hold more people. But of course, it was all the more appropriate to hold a service in the gym, where Mr. Rustin had spent so many hours.

Mr. Lonside spoke about Mr. Rustin. He told facts that none of us knew, such as where he was born and where he went to college. I didn't really care about where he had taught before he came to our school. But when he mentioned his wife and Carly, I found myself sniffing back tears once again.

Then Mr. Lonside asked Stephen to stand. He praised my brother for his quick actions the day before. Everyone burst into applause. Stephen was the school hero, even if he had not succeeded in reviving Mr. Rustin. But I could tell by looking at my brother that he did not feel like a hero. Looking at the grim expression on his face, I knew he was miserable. He was blaming himself for Mr. Rustin's death. I guess he felt that if he had done something more, something better, we wouldn't be having this assembly. Mr. Rustin would be in the gym, packing up the equipment for the last game of the season.

The big game had been scheduled for the next day. However, the principal announced that he had spoken with the county sports committee, and the game was being postponed for a week.

Mr. Lonside asked all the members of the team to stand. Somehow, they all looked a couple of inches shorter than they had the day before. They didn't look as if they had it in them to play a game of ring-around-the-rosy, much less the championship game.

"Next week, I want you fellows to go out and play your best," said Mr. Lonside. "It's not the way you imagined it. It's not how you expected it would be. But it's still the big game. And win or lose, it's what Mr. Rustin would have wanted all of you to do."

Spontaneously, we all stood at those words, and we cheered loudly. We cheered for the team; we cheered for the memory of Mr. Rustin; we cheered because we were still alive and well; we cheered because if we didn't, we'd begin crying all over again. And I especially cheered for Stephen, because, looking at his face with that awful expression on it, I wanted to remind him that he had done his best and that I loved him. Everyone loved him for what he had tried to do, even if he had failed. Still, it was not enough. For Stephen, the perfect *A* student, an *A* for effort could never be enough.

# NINE
## ✤ *Last Respects* ✤

OF COURSE WE all went to the funeral—Stephen and me and several hundred students from Hoover High. There was even a group of recent graduates who had been on Mr. Rustin's team last year or the year before. Many teachers had arranged coverage of their classes so they could attend. On one side of the funeral home, I saw a cluster of very tall men sitting together. I guessed they were Mr. Rustin's former teammates from his own basketball-playing days. Despite the fact that my father was in the midst of trying a case and my mother never missed a day of school, my parents attended the funeral, too. They were there out of sympathy for Mrs. Rustin and to support Stephen.

Stephen had continued to take Teddy Rustin's death harder than anyone. He moped around the house, hardly speaking. He didn't want to go to school. However, when our parents insisted, he took his backpack and boarded the school bus. I saw him at school, sitting in the cafeteria or outside the building, cutting classes when he should have been in his advanced physics class or honors English.

Ironically, in the couple of days before the funeral, the mailbox had been filled with college acceptance letters for Stephen—Yale, MIT, Princeton, the works.

He even got a personal letter from the chairman of the history department at Princeton, saying he was delighted to read Stephen's application and looked forward to having him major in history. Stephen should have been elated. He should have been running through the house calling out, "Mirabile dictu." But nothing seemed able to change his mood.

At the funeral, Mrs. Rustin looked pale but composed. I suppose she was still in a state of shock about the whole thing. I guess she felt as if she was living in the middle of a nightmare. Nevertheless, she still had to cook meals for her daughter and play games with her and put her to bed at night. My mother said that doing everyday chores probably helped her get through the days.

Carly looked her usual cuddly self. She was wearing her party dress and holding a new doll that someone had just given her. Seeing so many people gathered together, even though they were quiet and solemn, must have seemed like some sort of party to her. She was too young to understand what the whole thing was about.

Stephen's problem was that he understood only too well. I think what he couldn't understand was what had gone wrong when he applied his CPR skills. How had he failed his teacher? What should he have done that he hadn't? To someone who taught himself to read when he was four, who had skipped a grade when he was eight, had aced every exam he had ever taken, who never made mistakes, never failed, this was the worst possible kind of failure. And Stephen was not accustomed to failure. Too bad he hadn't failed an algebra test or two to give him a little practice.

In a couple of days, the Hoover Hoops would have their big game. But somehow, Mr. Rustin's death put a new perspective on things for me. What was a basketball game but a game, after all. It would be great for the team to win. But it wouldn't be the end of the world if they didn't. Combing my hair and getting dressed for the funeral, I'd looked at myself in the mirror and was ashamed about the way I had carried on a few weeks before. So what if I wear glasses? At least they enable me to see better. At least I'm around to see things. Teddy Rustin wasn't going to see anything—not his team winning or losing games, not his beautiful wife, not little Carly.

I sniffed and blinked my eyes. Whenever I thought of Carly, I felt like crying. Would she remember her father when she grew up?

When the funeral was over, my parents went off to work. Dad gave Stephen's arm a squeeze, and my mother risked embarrassing my brother by giving him a hug. It's awful to watch your parents become helpless. I could tell that they were concerned about Stephen's distress, but they didn't seem to know how to handle it. They had never had to *handle* anything regarding Stephen before. He was so perfect that there had never been any problems. Some parents have to deal with kids who experiment with drugs, or fail classes, or get into trouble. My parents never had those kinds of problems. The worst thing Stephen ever did was leave his room in a mess or play his stereo too loud. So now they seemed to be giving Stephen as much space as they could and hoping that everything would right itself.

"Come on," I said to Stephen after my mother had given me a hug, too. "There's a bus loading up outside." The school had sent several buses to transport the students and teachers back to Hoover.

Stephen walked along with me, but out of our parents' view, he said, "You go on without me, Sunny. There's no way I can sit through even half a day of classes."

"It's better than sitting at home by yourself," I told him.

"Tomorrow," said Stephen. "Not today."

"Okay. I'll go with you," I offered.

"No. I need to be alone," he insisted.

I looked at the pain in his face and I felt terrible. I didn't know what to do.

"Come on, Sunny. Let's get on this bus." It was my friend Ellie.

"Go ahead," said Stephen, giving me a little push. And so I found myself crowded onto the bus with other kids, who, apparently relieved that the solemnity of the funeral service was over, were laughing and joking and talking about getting some lunch. It didn't seem appropriate behavior to me. No wonder Stephen wanted to avoid school.

A bit later, as I was waiting on line to buy some lunch, Nancy Cummings came over to me and said, "Sunny, I need your help."

"Me?" I asked her. Of all the girls Stephen has dated, I like Nancy the best. She has striking dark hair and eyes and a great sense of humor.

"Steven called me last night and uninvited me to go to the senior prom with him," she said.

"Uninvited you?" I asked. "I can't believe it. I thought he really liked you. Did you have a fight or something?"

"No, nothing," said Nancy. "Actually, he said he didn't want to go to the prom. He said he wasn't going to take anyone else. He said he felt it was a superficial activity and that everyone made too much fuss about proms. Then he said he'd ask one of his friends to take me if I couldn't find another date. Why would I want to go to the prom with one of his friends? It's crazy." Nancy's face grew flushed as she spoke to me, and she looked on the verge of tears.

"Did you know he's thinking of taking time off and not going to college in the fall?" she asked me.

"Stephen said that?" Now I was really shocked. This was getting more and more serious by the minute.

"You have to talk to him," Nancy said.

"It's because of Mr. Rustin dying," I said. "He's been very upset." I paused, wondering what I should or could possibly do for Nancy. And even more important, what I could do for Stephen.

I bought a tuna fish sandwich and a container of

fruit punch. I only nibbled at the sandwich, out of habit. Lunchtime is when you are supposed to eat. However, I didn't have much appetite that day.

"What's with you, Sunny?" teased Ellie. "Are you back to dreaming of Curtis? Or is it someone else?"

"Who knows?" I shrugged. Even though Ellie's one of my best friends, I didn't know what to say to her.

I looked at the clock. It was just before one. I knew that Mrs. Wolpers, the guidance counselor, had office hours between one and two. Maybe she could give me some advice. Wasn't that what the school paid her to do?

I crumpled up the wrapper from my sandwich and finished up the punch. Then, even though there was another twenty minutes until my lunch period was over, I got up from the table.

"I'll see you later," I told Ellie and my other classmates at our table.

"Do you want to come shopping with me after school?" Ellie asked. "I need a pair of new shoes. I'm going to the mall."

"Not today," I told her. "I've got to go straight home." I was thinking of Stephen lying on his bed, staring at the ceiling, looking for the answers that weren't coming.

Then I felt bad that Ellie would think I was trying to avoid spending time with her. "Can you wait till tomorrow?" I suggested. "I could go with you then."

"Sure. Why not?" she replied.

"Good to see you, Sunny," said Mrs. Wolpers when I walked into the guidance office.

"It would be better if you saw my brother," I said. "He's really been upset about Mr. Rustin's death. I was wondering if you could talk to him."

"I've spoken with him twice," she told me. That was a surprise. Stephen hadn't mentioned it. But come to think of it, since he wasn't speaking much these days, he didn't mention anything.

"I realize that he feels more involved in this death than the other students because he was the one who administered the CPR," Mrs. Wolpers said.

"Yes, and he's never failed at anything before," I pointed out. "He doesn't know how to deal with this sort of situation. Look at his record. He's always been perfect."

"Everyone here at Hoover is extremely proud of him. We're proud of his academic record. We're proud of him as a human being. But the truth is, nobody's perfect," said Mrs. Wolpers gently, repeating the very words my father had used the evening of Mr. Rustin's death. "It's a hard way for him to find it out. But that's the truth. Everyone fails at one time or another—even Stephen."

When I left the guidance office, there was only one thing left for me to do. For the first time in my life, I cut classes and went home. I had to talk to Stephen.

# TEN
## *I Make a Phone Call*

WHEN I WALKED into the house, there was no sign of Stephen. It was just as I expected: He was holed up in his bedroom.

I knocked on the door. "Stephen, can I come in?" I asked.

I thought he'd wonder what I was doing home so early. But if he noticed, he didn't mention it. "Not now, Sunny. I'm busy," he said in a voice I hardly recognized.

Busy my foot. "Please," I begged.

"Later, kid," he said.

"I'm not a kid," I called to him behind the door. "Please. Please let me talk to you. You're taking everything too hard. You're not being fair to yourself."

"Sunny, I just don't want to talk about it. And certainly not with you. You're too young to understand."

"I *do* understand," I insisted, annoyed that Stephen was treating me like a little child. "That's why we need to talk."

"Sunny. Go away," said Stephen.

There's no lock on his bedroom door, so unless he had barricaded himself in with furniture, I could have just pushed the door open and barged in. But it wouldn't have been a good beginning to a calm, understanding conversation.

I went to my room and sat at my desk. What could I possibly do or say that would bring back the old happy, successful, confident, charming Stephen Marx? There has to be something or someone that can help him overcome his depression, I thought to myself. He wouldn't listen to me. He wouldn't listen to our parents. He wouldn't listen to Mrs. Wolper. I thought of phoning Mrs. Rustin. Maybe if she told him that it wasn't his fault and that she didn't blame him, he would believe her. But how could I call a woman on the afternoon of her husband's funeral and ask her to make my brother feel better? I couldn't possibly do that. Then I got another idea.

I went downstairs and took the telephone book. I turned the pages until I located the listing for the American Red Cross. I dialed the number and kept my fingers crossed that whoever answered would understand the seriousness of my call.

"Can I speak to the person in charge of giving the CPR courses?" I asked, hoping I sounded mature and not like a kid.

"Please hold," the voice at the other end said.

"Are you the person in charge of giving the CPR classes?" I asked the next voice that got on the line.

"No. I just book people for the next available course. There will be one given on May fourth. There are a couple of openings left. Do you wish to sign up for it?"

"No. No. I don't want to take the course now. I need to speak to the person who *gives* the course. Can you connect me to that person?"

"None of our instructors are here in the building at this time," she said.

"Well, when can I get to talk to one of them? Actually, I really want a particular one. The person who gave the course last winter. It was a man."

"What is this in reference to?" the voice asked me suspiciously.

"It's kind of personal," I said softly, hoping that Stephen wouldn't come down the stairs and overhear my conversation. "My brother took the course, and a few days ago when he used the CPR techniques that he learned, they didn't work. Mr. Rustin—that is, the victim—died. He's feeling very bad about it. Not Mr. Rustin. I mean my brother," I corrected myself. I must sound like an idiot, I thought. "And I hoped maybe the instructor could talk to my brother. I'm sure that it wasn't his fault. Some people must die even if they get CPR. Isn't that right? That not everyone who is given CPR survives?"

"Of course," said the woman on the phone. "Proper CPR techniques increase one's chances for survival, but they are not a guarantee."

"Well, I think it's very important that my brother hear that directly from the person who taught him in the course. He's feeling awful just now. Like a terrible failure. Like he killed the man he was trying to save."

"Oh no, honey. He shouldn't feel that way. You said last winter. Was it January? February?"

"January," I said, hoping I was right.

"January. Let me see. January...January."

Over the telephone line, I could hear pages

rustling. "There were four sessions given during January, and two of them were given by men."

"Tell me their names," I asked the woman. "Maybe I'll recognize the right one when I hear it."

"There was Abe Sussman, and the other was George DeAngeli."

"That's the one," I said when I heard the second name. I was relieved that I remembered. "Mr. DeAngeli. Could you give me his number?"

"I'm not permitted to do that," the woman told me. "But I can contact him and let him get in touch with you. Tell me your name and number."

I gave her the information. "If he doesn't call today, tell him I'm in every day in the late afternoon and all evening. But it would be really great if he could call right away. Tell him it's awfully important."

"Okay, Allison," the woman replied. "I'll give him your message."

"Thanks a lot," I said gratefully. Now I just had to hope she could reach Mr. DeAngeli and that he would call me back.

I was lucky. In less than half an hour, the phone rang. It was Mr. DeAngeli. I explained everything to him. "You have to speak to my brother," I said. "He's blaming himself for what happened. I'm sure it wasn't his fault that his coach died."

"I remember Steve," said Mr. DeAngeli. "Most of the people who take the course are older—adults who need the certification for their jobs or women worrying about their husbands' health. So Steve stood out as being different, taking the course as a public ser-

vice and as a self-motivated young man. He was an earnest and thoughtful student. He even helped a couple of people who were having difficulties remembering what to do."

The Stephen he described was my old brother, not the one who was sitting upstairs in his bedroom just then.

"Could you come and talk to him? Explain to him that it's okay that he didn't save Mr. Rustin's life? I mean, it's not okay, but it's not what Stephen did or didn't do that caused the death."

"Well, it's a bit unorthodox," Mr. DeAngeli said. "I don't think I've ever run into this sort of situation before."

"Please. Please," I begged him. "It's very important that you speak to my brother." I thought of something. "I could pay you. I have some money from baby-sitting."

"No, no," said Mr. DeAngeli. "You can give a contribution to the Red Cross, if you want. I'm giving a class this evening, but I'm free at the moment. Would it be convenient if I came now?"

"Oh, that would be great," I said excitedly. I gave him our address, and he said he lived in the next town. "I'll be at your home within twenty minutes," he promised.

I sat down on the sofa, thrilled with the success of my phone calls. I had no doubt that Mr. DeAngeli was the one person who could best make Stephen come to terms with his failure to save Mr. Rustin.

Five minutes after I hung up the phone, Stephen came downstairs. I looked at him to see if I could tell from his expression whether or not he had overheard me on the telephone. But his eyes still had that dead expression that they'd had for the past three days.

"See you later," he said. "I'm going for a walk."

"Oh no, you can't," I said.

"What's with you, Sunny?" he asked. "Of course I can go for a walk."

I thought fast. Anytime in the past, I would have told Stephen exactly what was what. That Mr. DeAngeli was on his way over. That he should remain at home and wait for him. But the new Stephen was different from the old one. I was afraid that he'd be angry at me if he knew what I'd done. He might not stay home. I had to think quickly and come up with a reason to keep Stephen in the house.

"Well...well, I think I smell smoke," I said. "So don't leave me. The house may be on fire."

Stephen sniffed the air. "I don't smell anything," he said. "You must be imagining it."

"No," I said. "I think maybe it's coming from the basement. But I'm afraid to go down and check. Please do it for me."

Stephen sighed. But he started down the steps to the basement. "Maybe there's something wrong with the furnace," I called after him. I looked at my watch. Mr. DeAngeli wouldn't be at the house for at least another ten minutes, maybe more. Maybe there would be traffic. Maybe he wasn't dressed when I spoke to him. Maybe he needed to shave before he left the house. Maybe he stopped for a bite to eat.

For one moment, I thought of closing the basement door behind Stephen and fastening it shut. There was an old hook and eye on the door, left over from when I was a little kid. My parents used it to keep the door shut so I wouldn't fall down the basement steps.

No, I thought. That's stupid. I can't lock my brother down in the basement. Even as I made that decision, Stephen came up the steps and walked into the kitchen. "There's no odor of smoke in the basement or in the kitchen," he said. "You must be hallucinating."

"Well, come with me and we'll check the rest of the house," I pleaded.

"Oh, Sunny. You're crazy," he said. But he led the way up the stairs and we began a "search" for a possible source of smoke.

Of course, there was nothing. So thinking quickly, I pretended to trip as we were going back down the stairs.

"Ooooh," I moaned. "I think I sprained my ankle."

"What's with you today, Sunny?" Stephen asked. "Smelling nonexistent smells, acting like a klutz."

"Help me to the sofa," I demanded. I leaned heavily on his arm as I hobbled across the room.

"Take off your shoe and sock," he said. "Let's see if your ankle is getting swollen."

Of course, my ankle wasn't swollen. It wasn't red. There was nothing.

"It hurts when I try to move it," I said, pretending to wince at the pain as I twisted my ankle about. "Get some ice. That's what I need. If I put ice on my ankle, it will prevent it from swelling."

"Do you honestly expect me to believe your ankle is sprained?" Stephen asked me. "It looks perfectly fine to me."

I had the feeling that Stephen was seeing through my antics. But I couldn't give up now. "It's killing me. The pain is awful," I lied. "Please. Please get me some ice."

Mumbling under his breath with annoyance, Stephen went into the kitchen to get ice. I glanced again at my watch. We had killed another ten minutes, and I was exhausted. I was also ready to be nominated for an Academy Award. All this playacting was hard work.

"Here," said Stephen. He gave me some ice cubes wrapped in a dish towel.

"Oh," I exclaimed as I placed it on my ankle. "It's so cold."

"Ice usually is," said Stephen dryly.

"I think I need a drink of water. And maybe an aspirin for the pain," I added.

I was already thinking that next I'd ask him to make me a sandwich, but then the doorbell rang. Thank goodness for that.

Stephen went to answer the door. I could hear the surprise in his voice as he greeted the gray-haired man in the entryway. Then they walked into the living room.

"Mr. DeAngeli, this is my sister, Allison, but we all

call her Sunny. Sunny, this is Mr. DeAngeli. He taught the CPR class that I took."

"Hi," I said, smiling sheepishly.

"Do you know anything about sprains?" Stephen asked Mr. DeAngeli. "Sunny tripped coming down the stairs, and she says her ankle hurts."

"Oh. I'm fine now," I said, jumping up. "Look. I can move my ankle just fine."

"A miraculous recovery," said Stephen, raising his eyebrows. "And what about the smoke?"

"What smoke?" I asked him.

"The smoke that you told me you could smell. The smoke you said indicated that our house was burning down."

"I guess you were right," I said, not looking at Stephen but busily putting my sock and sneaker back on. "I must have imagined it."

"Or made it up," suggested Stephen.

"Why would you say that?" I asked in my best Academy Award voice.

"Because you know and I know that we have four smoke detectors around this house. There is no way you're going to smell any smoke before one of those alarms goes off."

"Oh," I said. "So you knew I was making it up all along."

"Yeah," said Stephen.

I was so embarrassed. I looked over at Mr. DeAngeli. "I must sound like a compulsive liar," I said to him. "But one thing is true. Stephen needs to talk to you. Tell him about why Mr. Rustin died. Tell him that it's not his fault."

Then I ran out of the room, using my two perfectly fine ankles. The ball was in Mr. DeAngeli's court now. I just hoped he was up to the job.

# ELEVEN
## ❖ *Sunny Days* ❖

I WISH I could say that at supper that evening Stephen was his old self. He wasn't. He probably would never be the same carefree kid he'd been before. On the other hand, I'd changed, too. We were both older and more thoughtful. We'd learned a lot about life and ourselves in the past few days.

Still, Stephen sat and ate with us. That was a start. And afterward, he suggested that I go for a walk with him. I knew that was a good sign, too.

It was one of those April evenings when the scent of spring is in every breath you take. In the dim evening light, I looked up and saw the tree branches with the beginnings of new leaves. The azalea bushes were just coming into bloom in the front yards along our street. Soon the block would be ablaze with the red and bright pink bushes. I took a deep breath. It smelled great to be alive!

I didn't know what to say, so I waited for Stephen to talk first.

"You're really amazing," he said to me, after we'd walked in silence for a couple of minutes. "I can't believe you arranged for Mr. DeAngeli to come here. How in the world did you find him?"

"Where there's a will, there's a way," I said, quoting an old saying my math teacher sometimes uses. Of course, it doesn't always seem to apply to me and algebra at all. Although there was no longer any doubt that I'd pass the course.

"What did Mr. DeAngeli say to you?" I asked.

"Well, to begin with, he told me in much more detail than he'd gone into in the CPR class what the chances are of saving someone's life. When a person receives cardiopulmonary resuscitation, it greatly increases their chances for survival—but it's not a guarantee. Then, he actually phoned the hospital where we took Mr. Rustin and spoke with someone on the staff there. Because they know Mr. DeAngeli, they checked the records for him. They affirmed what we had already heard, that Mr. Rustin suffered a massive heart attack—the kind from which there is no return. It could have happened in his sleep. It could have happened the day before. It could have happened next month. Apparently without his being aware of it, he had a serious heart condition. That meant it was a trauma waiting to happen. Mr. DeAngeli said there was no way on earth that I, or he, or anyone could have saved poor Teddy Rustin when he collapsed in the gym."

"So now you know it isn't your fault that he died," I said, relieved that Stephen had been made to understand what I had realized on my own.

"I guess I knew all along it wasn't my fault," Stephen admitted. "But somehow, I felt so helpless. I thought I'd be able to save him. And when I couldn't, I just went to pieces."

"And now, are you back together again?" I asked.

"I guess so," said Stephen. "But it just seems so unfair. Teddy Rustin still had his whole life ahead of him. And now he's gone. Just like that." Stephen snapped his fingers.

"But what he had was good," I pointed out. "He loved his work coaching the team. He was proud of all you guys. He had a loving family. Some people live a whole lot longer and don't have as much."

Stephen nodded his head.

I didn't know if it was too soon to ask, but I thought I'd better do it while I had a chance. "Stephen," I said.

"Yeah?"

"What are you going to do about college? I saw Nancy at school today. She said you were thinking of taking time off," I reported.

"I was thinking about it, but I've changed my mind."

I let out a sigh of relief. I couldn't imagine Stephen not going on with his education. "So you'll be off to Harvard? Or are you going to Princeton?" I asked.

"No, neither," Stephen admitted.

"Yale?"

"I've decided to go to Haverford. That's where Dad went, after all. It's smaller, but it has a great reputation, even if it isn't as well known."

"No kidding?" I was really surprised by Stephen's unexpected choice, but I had a feeling that Dad would be thrilled. "I guess a lot of wait-listed students at all those other schools are going to be very happy about your decision." I thought of the seniors who would be getting letters from the colleges that Stephen turned down. There was a place for them now that Stephen wasn't going to take it.

I thought of something else. "When I saw Nancy, she also told me that you're not going to take her to the senior prom. She was looking forward to going to that dance with you."

"A prom seems such a silly thing, after an event like this."

"I know," I agreed. "But I bet Mr. Rustin took someone to the prom when he was in high school. It was part of what made up his life. I bet he'd want you to go. I bet he'd want Carly to go, too, when she grows up."

"You may be right," he admitted.

"Do me a favor?" I asked him.

"Yeah?"

"Go over to Nancy's house. Talk to her."

"Now?"

"Sure. I'm a big girl. I can walk home alone. I'm not afraid of the dark," I reminded him.

"Well, okay," said Stephen. "I do feel pretty bad about the way I've been handling things the last few days."

So in the end, Stephen and Nancy went to the high school prom. But that wasn't until a few other events took place first. The Hoover Hoops won the county championship but lost in the statewide competition. And Stephen put together a double page in the school paper in tribute to Teddy Rustin. He gathered all the photos anyone could dig up and made a montage of them. He asked students to write little memorial pieces about things they remembered. Even though I'm always reluctant to expose my written thoughts, I felt I should submit something, too.

I had a hard time pulling all my thoughts together. I hardly knew Mr. Rustin, but I'd heard Stephen talking about him so often, I felt as if I did. And because of my connection as their baby-sitter, in some ways I knew the Rustins better than anyone else. After all, sitting in their living room, I'd seen the family pictures displayed on the top shelf of their bookcase. I may have been the only one in the school who had seen the framed photograph of Mr. and Mrs. Rustin on their wedding day, or the picture of the young, but still recognizable to me, Teddy Rustin and a man I guessed was his father, posing proudly with the fish they had caught.

I tore up about a hundred sheets of paper before I figured out what I should write. I wrote an open letter to Carly, telling her what a great father she had. It was only three paragraphs long and I wasn't sure Stephen would accept it for the paper—even if I am his sister and he's the type of brother to go out of his way to be kind.

When the memorial issue came out, my letter was in a box with a black border around it in the center of the spread. Loads of students came up to me in the halls to say how my letter had made them cry. But the most unexpected thing was when Lisa Schmidt, the assistant editor, who is going to be editor of the paper next year, approached me.

"I should have guessed that anyone related to Stephen would be a great writer," she said.

"No," I said. "I'm not really great at anything. I just do my best."

"Your best is pretty good. How would you like to write for the paper next year?" she asked.

"Really? You mean be a reporter?" I could hardly believe it. After all, Lisa isn't related to me. She didn't have to make such an offer.

"Anyone can be a reporter. I thought you might like to have your own column. I know everyone calls you Sunny. You could call it 'Sunny Days' and write about whatever you want—some issue at school, or something in the news, a movie or book review from time to time, anything at all."

"Wow. I'd love to." I could hardly believe what she was offering me.

"Great. Consider yourself a member of next year's staff," said Lisa.

The evening of the senior prom, Stephen looked smashing, almost like a movie star. He wore a rented black tuxedo, with a bright red cummerbund (that's a kind of sash) around his waist. And Nancy wore a bright red dress. It was short. I've always imagined that when I go to the prom, if someone asks me, I'll wear a long, flowing dress. But now that I've seen Nancy, I'm not sure.

Stephen and Brian and Curtis rented a limo, and everyone on our street was watching when the enormous white car pulled up in front of our house.

"Do you feel bad that things didn't work out between you and Curtis?" Stephen asked me.

"No way," I said, and I meant it. I wouldn't have the energy to make conversation through another whole evening with Curtis Silvers. I've learned that personality is as important as looks in a boyfriend. In fact, I'd say it's more important. So there, Curtis Silvers!

When the limo pulled up, Brian and Curtis and their dates, as well as Nancy, were already in the car. They all got out so my dad could take pictures of them. Both Curtis's and Brian's dates were wearing black. I looked Curtis's date over carefully. She didn't go to our school, so I didn't recognize her. I hoped she was good at talking to a tree.

I had suggested to Stephen that the students raise money for a scholarship fund for Carly. So, in addition to a raffle and a cake sale and a car wash and all the other usual fund-raising events that Hoover High traditionally does to make money, Stephen came up with a great plan. None of the guys bought corsages for their dates. Instead, each one, on his honor, donated the amount of money he would have spent on flowers to the fund. In all, we raised several thousand dollars toward Carly's college education.

As for Stephen's education, he's decided that instead of going on to law school, he wants to go to medical school when he completes college. He's thinking of specializing in cardiology.

"It's a scary specialty," he admitted to me. "I'll be working with some very ill patients along the way. But

I'm going to work hard and do my best by them. Maybe I'll be able to improve the quality of their lives and prevent heart attacks."

"You could always become a dermatologist," I pointed out. "No one ever dies of acne."

"I don't think that would be challenging enough," said Stephen. "So I'll have to live with the risks."

He sounded to me like the confident brother I had always known.

So now Stephen is off in Pennsylvania. Nancy is at college in Washington. And Curtis is somewhere in Massachusetts. And I'm still here. I have three more years of high school. It's plenty of time to improve my math skills and make new friends and write my newspaper columns. Ellie drew a funny caricature of me with my long, curly blond hair and my big eyeglass frames, and it's printed at the top of my column. It's funny how in just a few lines she actually captured me. And looking at it, I realize that those glasses are part of my identity—sort of the way Groucho Marx's eyebrows and cigar were part of his image.

I've been sending copies of the column to Stephen, and he seems to really like them.

Yesterday, I got a letter from him. This is what it said:

Dear Sunny,
    Your columns get better and better. They are
fun to read and they make me think and laugh.

In fact, all my roommates read your last column after they found me laughing aloud over it. They enjoyed it, too. Eric—the guy from Oregon that I told you about—says he wants to meet my little sister when you and Mom and Dad come for parents' weekend next month. I told him that the columns are just like you.

You probably think that you got the nickname you have because it's short for Allison or because of all that curly blond hair that covers your head. But the truth is that by being yourself, you bring a bit of sunshine into the lives of everyone you touch.

I sat reading Stephen's letter over and over and over again. It's what makes a letter more special than a telephone call. If he had said those words on the phone, I'd probably have managed to convince myself afterward that I'd imagined the whole thing. But there it was on paper—the very best compliment I ever got. It felt good to be alive and good to be me. I wouldn't trade with anyone—even Stephen.

## ABOUT THE AUTHOR

Johanna Hurwitz is the award-winning author of many popular books for young readers, including the Beech Tree paperbacks *Anne Frank: Life in Hiding, Baseball Fever, Birthday Surprises: Ten Great Stories to Unwrap,* and *Tough-Luck Karen*. She has received a number of child-chosen state awards, including the Texas Bluebonnet Award, the Kentucky Bluegrass Award, and the Garden State Children's Book Award. A former children's librarian, Mrs. Hurwitz travels around the country to visit schools and discuss books with students, teachers, parents, and librarians. She lives with her husband in Great Neck, New York, and Wilmington, Vermont.